DEATH AMONG THE STARS

BY C. M. LOCKHART

WRITTEN IN MELANIN

Established • 2019

THE LADY WIDOW

BOOK 1

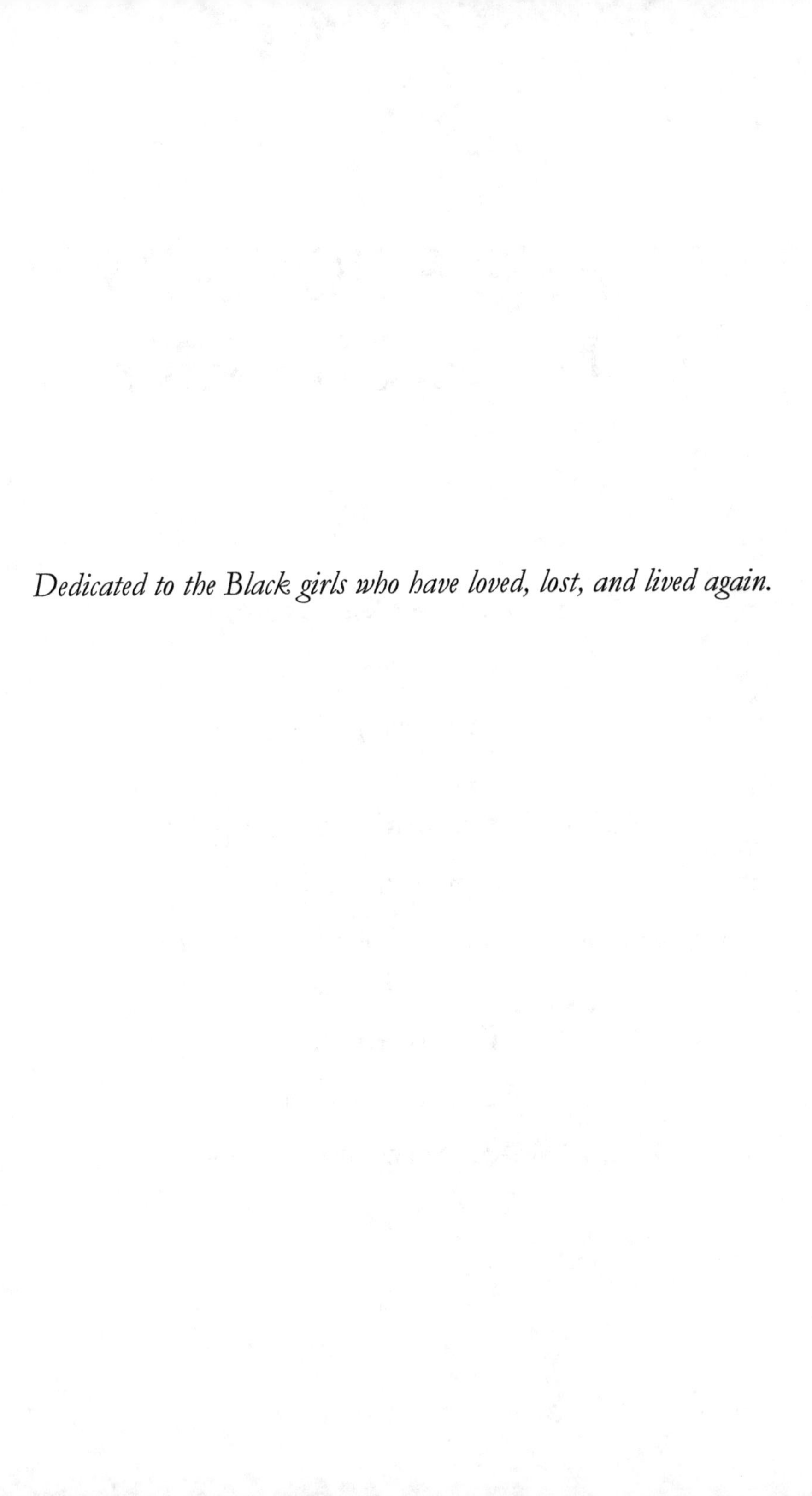

Dedicated to the Black girls who have loved, lost, and lived again.

OTHER BOOKS BY C. M. LOCKHART

Wrath of the Gods Trilogy

We Are the Origin

We Are Dying Gods

Standalones and Anthologies

Keeping Promises

Magic in the Melanin: A Black Fantasy Anthology

Featured in

The Stygian Collection

FIYAH #32: Spacefaring Aunties

AUTHOR'S NOTE

Dear reader,

Thank you for picking up The Lady Widow. This book is a novella and the first book in a series about a grieving widow who becomes an intergalactic bounty hunter to avenge her husband's murder. It deals with themes of death, grief, and substance abuse (smoking), so please be mindful of that before beginning this story. Also, this is a story of unapologetic revenge — there is murder involved. So, please make the decision that is best for you and your mental health. An updated list of content warnings will be kept on my website at CMLockhart.com.

Enjoy.

BİRTH OF A WİDOW

I died on a Thursday.

Not in the literal sense, but in every way that mattered. My heart, my hope, my future — everything that made me who I was lay rotting in the ground, next to Xavier's corpse. And part of me wanted to laugh at the irony of him dying before me. He'd traveled to countless galaxies. Had seen beautiful worlds and talked to people in languages I couldn't even fathom. For centuries.

Centuries.

He was supposed to far outlive my puny lifespan, and yet here I was, staring at the upturned soil of his freshly filled grave.

"This is not what I had in mind when we agreed 'til death do us part'," I whispered, staring at the cold stone that marked everything that was left of who Xavier had been. I tried to take a deep breath, but my chest was full — packed to the brim with thoughts and emotions too difficult to sort through — and it came out in shuddering halts as I dug my teeth into my bottom lip. "But I guess our promises don't matter anymore, do they?"

Part of me waited for a response. Prayed for one. As if he'd walk out from behind a tree with a grin and an apology for making me worry. And I swore to the universe that if he did — if this reality could be turned into nothing more than a suffocating night terror — I'd forgive him. But there was only silence. And the wind rushing through the cemetery. It drowned out my uneven breaths and brought with it the thick scent of rain.

Goosebumps trailed up my arms, and I focused on the chill in the breeze rather than the ice forming in my veins. It was better that way. Easier.

"How long are you going to stand there?"

I looked up at James and couldn't even muster the energy to glare at him.

"As long as I feel like it."

I returned my eyes to the stone in front of us with Xavier's name carved into it, but I felt James' gaze bore into the side of my face. I knew my words were sharper than necessary, but what kind of question was that to ask a woman who'd just buried her husband? It brewed something bitter in my chest, and I gnawed on my bottom lip as my face tightened and I swallowed against the burning ache in my throat.

James said nothing as he stood beside me, his looming frame casting mine in shadow. He lifted an umbrella over us with one hand and pressed a cigarette to his lips with the other. He lit it and sucked in a deep breath of the acrid smoke before blowing it away from me as the first drops of rain plopped down around us.

"I didn't mean it like that," he said, offering the words as a pathetic apology as he let out a deep sigh and rubbed a hand over his bald head. "I just… you can't stand here forever."

"Watch me."

"Ky…" he let my name trail off and shook his head. "We're leaving tomorrow," he stated, tapping out another cigarette from the pack and offering it to me. I stared at it.

"Have a safe trip," I said.

"You coming with us?"

I turned his question over in my mind as I gave in to his silent offer, breathing in as I dipped the cigarette into the flame he clicked to life. I held the smoke in my lungs, letting it burn the inside of my chest and scratch up the back of my throat in familiar ways before blowing it out and watching it disappear in the foggy downpour.

Xavier had loved the stars. Had promised to show them to me. Had woven countless stories of his adventures and begged me to go with him on his next one.

But he lived in my world, and I was never ready to be in his.

There was work. My dad. Work. Jasmine and her new baby. Work. Laundry.

Work.

There was always something that needed my attention more than he did, and I'd believed I had time. All the time.

Until I had none.

So, what did it matter now? Our home was just a house, and I was already tired of haunting it.

"Sure," I said, breathing out another stream of smoke as I stared down at the headstone.

"The ship is at Emerald Isle. We leave at dawn."

"Sure," I said again, tapping the ash away. "I'll be ready."

8 DAYS A WIDOW

"Welcome aboard *The Reveler*, Lady Kyra," James said, waving his hand around the control center. "Our crew is at your command."

"My command?" I asked, lifting an eyebrow at him before letting my gaze slide over the blinking lights and shifting screens. Five seats formed a crescent behind the consoles in the center of the room and James introduced the three people sitting at them as the triplets, though they were of no relation — Karmen, Keelah, Kavira. Their eyes were slitted into glares with varying levels of distrust and unabashed disdain, but I didn't waste my attention on them.

It was my first time inside Xavier's ship, and it was nothing like what I'd imagined it would be. The matte black orb was like a small city on the inside — dozens of times bigger than what seemed possible from the outside, and I was overwhelmed.

It was like walking through the heart of a busy city.

The control center was near the top of the ship, situated in the center of the third floor, or Sector 3, as James had called it. It was a pitch-black sphere connected by two walkways that hovered in the center of an atrium.

It was like a tiny sanctuary.

Outside was loud — crowded. The wide hallways from Sector 4 down to Sector 9 were filled with people rushing around with last-minute tasks before departure. But walking through the automatic doors into the control room stripped me of my anxiety and placed me in the midst of someone else's heartbeat — it dropped me into a slow and steady rhythm that forced me to keep pace with it.

It was tranquil.

Like falling into a quiet snow globe.

Or stepping into a crystal marble. I saw the world on all sides — from the ocean waves in the distance to the gray skies above us, to the footsteps James and I had left in the sand.

It was incredible, and my eyes prickled when I remembered that Xavier had tried to show me this. And I hated myself for refusing his offers. For being too scared of getting swept up in one of his adventures. For thinking we would always have more time.

"Xavier left this ship and crew to you," James said, his words gentle as he edged closer to me, his hands reaching out as if I were a toddler taking her first steps — unsure of whether he should catch me before I fall or give me the chance to run.

And somehow, that pissed me off. As if he would be strong enough for me to lean on. My glare must've said as much, because he pulled his hands back, shoving them into his pockets as he shrugged.

"He wanted you to see the stars."

"Then he should've lived long enough to take me to them."

The words were sour — bitter on my tongue — and my mouth recoiled from the taste of them. Even I knew they were unreasonable, but I refused to take them back as I stepped away from James, scoffing at the pity glazing over his face.

In another life, I would've apologized for snapping at him. Because he didn't deserve my hostility. I knew that. But here he was. Six-eight, with charcoal skin, blacker-than-night eyes, and a bald head — looking just like Xavier. Walking around, alive and well, when my husband was in the ground. And that seemed like an unforgivable offense. Because why was he the one who came back?

I hated myself for thinking that. But I couldn't shake it either. The thought had taken up residence in my brain like it paid rent to be there ever since James had shown up on my doorstep, telling me Xavier would never return. I didn't hate James for coming back. Just that he came back without Xavier. And my chest tightened thinking about the moment. But I refused to fall apart — not now. Not in front of strangers. Not in front of anyone. Not ever. So, I glared at him instead, and his dark gaze softened as if he deserved my rage and accepted it without question.

"I agree," he said. "But the fact remains that Xavier is gone, and you are the captain now." He offered me a weak smile too full of hope, and I shook my head, the back of my throat burning as I swallowed against the tide of emotions that rose at the sound of Xavier's name.

"I'm no one's captain," I said, hiking my duffel bag higher on my shoulder. It still shocked me how easy it had been to shove my entire life into it. Now that Xavier was gone, I realized there weren't many material things in life worth clinging to. "I'm just along for the ride."

"Then we have your permission to depart?"

"Sure," I said, tossing the word over my shoulder as I turned to leave. The door to the control room hissed open. "Take me wherever you want to go."

"You settling in okay?"

I glanced over to James and shrugged as he let himself into the room. It was a tiny space with nothing but the bare bones of necessity — a single bed, a desk that doubled as a nightstand, and an uncomfortable-looking chair in front of it. Two doors on the wall to the right led to a closet and a bathroom.

"I guess."

I tossed the words at him before returning my gaze to the display panels that served as windows. The room was an interior one, but like in the control center, display panels littered the walls inside of the ship. They gave everyone an unrestricted view of the void of space outside. There was a ledge at just the right height to lean on, and I hadn't moved from the spot since laying claim to the room.

That was the extent of my "settling in". And James seemed to notice, but what did he expect? That I'd be playing with the customization panel on the wall — swiping through all the designs and requesting to add curtains and rugs and art and color to the walls? None of that mattered to me. I barely even wanted to turn on the light. But I could see wrinkles forming between his brows, so before he could open his mouth, I rolled my eyes.

"Bathroom's nice," I offered.

And it was. The shower was separate from the tub, and the tub was more than big enough for my five-nine frame to sink into the water up to my chin and stretch my legs out with room to spare. It was self-cleaning, filled with the touch of a button, had a million options for aromatherapy scents, and could keep the water warm for hours. Heated floors, towel warmers, lighted mirrors, and bath bombs galore — it was a mini paradise. There were display panels embedded into the ceiling too, offering a constant view of the shifting stars we flew through. If I wasn't trapped in the icy grip of abject misery, I might've been excited about it.

Maybe.

"Good," he said, nodding. "And if you ever change your mind about —"

"I won't," I said, cutting him off. "You can have the room."

"I have my own room already," James countered. "And I'm not the captain."

James had tried to give me the Captain's Quarters — the giant room around the corner from the control center in Sector 3. But the moment the doors had hissed open, I knew I wouldn't be able to stay there. Every micro-inch of that space was steeped in Xavier's presence, and I just couldn't do it. From the navy blue decor to the soft rugs, giant bed, pictures of us on the nightstand, and his clothes still hanging in the closet, it had all been too much. But the hardest part was the smell. The entire room smelled like his cologne — as if he'd just stepped out for a moment and would be back any second — and I'd bolted down the corridor like I was back in high school, running track.

James found me a few moments later, trembling in an empty stall of the bathroom. I could only imagine what I'd looked like — head in my hands, trying not to hyperventilate. He'd approached me like I was a wild animal — cornered and feral.

And maybe I was.

But he'd taken me to the other side of the ship and given me my pick of the rooms. I'd chosen an empty one at the lowest possible level of the ship in Sector 9. It was at the end of a long hallway most everyone else considered to be a dead end. There was a single door at the end that led to Sector 10, which was restricted to authorized personnel only. Aside from the engineers, mechanics, and shipwrights — who all served different purposes aboard *The Reveler* — the hallway by my room didn't get much foot traffic.

I preferred that.

I'd just taken a seat on the bed when a soft voice overhead announced we were taking off. I'd expected it to be a more jarring experience, like I'd seen in movies — with the entire crew strapped down, buttons glowing, orders shouted and the whole ship shaking as we braced ourselves to leave the atmosphere or stratosphere or whatever you called it. But it had been a seamless transition.

I was pretty sure I was the only one who stopped to bear witness to the moment — the only one who stared at the display panels and ascribed any meaning to watching Earth shrink away as we were swallowed by the gaping maw of the universe. It was just Star Prime 1307 to everyone else, but to me, it was the home I'd never return to. Part of me almost wanted to feel nostalgic at the thought. But what was home if I was the only one who remembered it?

What was a memory worth if there was no one to share it with?

Absolutely nothing if anyone were to ask me.

It's a tragedy that no one did.

"I already told you —"

"Whether you want the title or not is irrelevant," James said, cutting off my rebuttal. "Either you die and pass along the mantle, or you disband the crew and retire the ship," he said, his voice hard. "Until then, you are the captain."

I turned to meet his unyielding gaze and sighed, shaking my head. James could be more stubborn than Xavier when he wanted to be, and I had no interest in arguing with him.

"Doesn't matter. I'm comfortable here."

"You could've brought more, you know," he said, glancing over to the open door of the closet — bare, save for my tiny black duffel bag that sat at the bottom.

"I brought what I needed."

James nodded and said nothing else. Instead, he moved to lean against the wall next to the doorway. His presence was almost a familiar comfort. If I kept my eyes closed and let go of my tenuous grip on reality, I could almost pretend that he was Xavier. Could almost delude myself into thinking this nightmare wasn't real, and Xavier was the one standing on the other side of the room. But dreams were fleeting, and I would never be able to warp reality to my whims. And James would never be able to replace Xavier.

He couldn't.

"You know you can always talk to me if you need to, Ky."

His words were soft. Gentle. They didn't match the deep baritone of his voice at all. And while I knew he meant to offer me comfort — to let me know that I wasn't alone — his words felt like a knife twisting through my soul, cutting through the core of my being. I'd always known they were similar — they were from the same planet — but right now, he was too much like Xavier.

Too kind. Too concerned.

It was too cruel to have an almost-but-not-quite version of my husband standing in my room, offering me a shoulder to lean on. What kind of unusual torture was this? I couldn't stand to be around him, and I wanted nothing more than for James to take his leave and never come back. But I couldn't say that. So, I endured his presence. But breathing became an insurmountable challenge, and I shook my head.

"There's really nothing to talk about," I whispered.

"There's plenty to talk about," he said, coughing out a dry laugh. "But I guess it doesn't have to be now."

"Or ever," I muttered.

"But when you're ready, know that I'm here," he said, ignoring my slick remark. "I promised Zay to look after you, and I intend to keep my word."

"You come all the way down here just to tell me that?"

"Yes," he said, nodding before pushing off the wall. "And to give you these."

He reached into the inside pocket of his leather jacket and pulled out a box of matches. For a moment, I expected him to offer me another cigarette, but before I could fix my mouth to decline, he was tossing the matches over to me. They landed on the bed next to me with a soft thump. He stepped outside to the hallway and returned with a tiny orange sphere.

It was more of a blob than anything else.

"What is that?"

James answered with a set of sounds I couldn't comprehend. And when I stared at him, blinking with vacant brown eyes, he offered me a small smile.

"We call them slimes. And this one's a fire-eater," he said, striking a match. "Feed it fire, and it blows out smoke."

"And why would I want that?"

Before James had a chance to respond, the little blob glubbed and sweet smoke filled my lungs. I was instantly wrapped in a cocoon of fresh snow, burning wood, and toasted marshmallows on graham crackers. The scent reminded me of snow days when I was a child, and for the briefest moment, I could breathe again. I wasn't suffocated by grief, and I wanted to cry as I sucked in a deep breath for the first time in what felt like years.

It was temporary, but even a momentary reprieve felt like heaven.

James kept talking, but his words were lost on me. They sounded like terms and conditions, and just like I had back home, I agreed to them without ever really knowing what they were. All I knew was that he was more than happy to relinquish the slime to me when I reached for it and I squished it close to my chest.

"Don't forget what I said," he warned as he headed toward the doorway.

"Sure."

"I'll drop off some more matches later with the translator I mentioned," he said, nodding.

"Translator?"

"Weren't you listening?" he asked, pausing by the door. "There's only a handful of us who speak your language, so…" he stared my face, at my eyes glazing over, and shook his head. "Just put on the earpiece I give you. Don't take it off unless you have to."

"Sure."

"And if you need me, Ky, just shout. I'm not Xavier, but I'll still come running."

"Thanks," I whispered, turning away from him and placing the glob on the window ledge next to me. "But I won't."

20 DAYS A WIDOW

The days blurred together, and I hated them all.

The ship became a prison. Everywhere I went, there was nothing but looks of doubt and pity, and I could only imagine what everyone thought of the poor human woman on the ship.

So, that's the wife?

What's wrong with her?

Why did the captain choose her?

It was sickening.

Less than two weeks aboard *The Reveler* and I'd already grown to regret my decision to leave the tiny blue dot I hailed from. Somewhere in my mind, I'd thought it would be better to be around people who'd known him — loved him. I'd convinced myself that anything would be better than living in our cold, empty house on my own.

But I was wrong.

I'd underestimated their disappointment. I was a stranger to them, and that was an unforgivable sin. Their betrayal was just as raw as my own emotions, and I couldn't fault them for detesting me. I was the last person to carry the heart of their beloved captain, and they didn't know me.

And that was my fault.

The guilt wore on me, and with each passing moment, it became exceptionally clear that I should've just let myself be buried with Xavier. At least then I could have gone out with some dignity rather than being relegated to Xavier's last dalliance.

Because that's all they saw me as. Not his wife. Not his lover. Not the woman he'd sworn to take to the stars and keep at his side until her dying breath. I was just a detour.

An entanglement.

A side quest he conquered in between traversing solar systems.

So, even in my most desperate moments, I didn't dare reach out to anyone. There was no hope I'd be saved from my isolation — not when the rest of the crew averted their gazes from mine whenever our eyes met. Not when they lowered their voices to heavy whispers when they passed me in the halls. Not when James was the only one who cared to speak more than two words to me on any given day. I was an outsider infiltrating a sacred space and knowing that was how they saw me was infuriating. It made me despise every moment that brought me to boarding *The Reveler* without Xavier.

I should've stayed home.

The only saving grace in this self-inflicted torture chamber was the observatory. At the very top of the ship — beyond the residences, greenhouse, library, and central hub — in an inconspicuous corner of Sector 1, was a tiny loft with a bench. It was just big enough for two people to sit on — three if they were packed in together. It was covered in navy blue cushions, had no back to it, and the only thing to do in that tiny space was sit on that bench and stare out of the giant window panel that spanned the entire wall in front of it — watching the stars as *The Reveler* passed by them.

A tiny radio was always left on in the furthest corner. It played sweet, melodic sounds with words I never understood, but I never moved to turn it off — never tried to change the station. It was peaceful in its own way, and I just melted into the sounds.

Two sides of the platform curved into the upper dome of the ship. The left edge was left open so that anyone could peer over it, but the gravity control on the ship kept anyone from falling to their deaths.

I'd seen some of the kids in the central hub jumping from the edges of Sectors 4 and 5 — throwing themselves over the edge with abandon and laughter. Screaming and falling and giggling until they slowed to a stop at Sector 9. From what I could tell, the gravity control on the ship was nuanced. There was the constant control that kept all of us on our feet instead of floating around, some modified control for specific rooms and sectors, and the safety protocols that kept anyone from falling — or jumping — to their deaths in the atrium. It was wild to watch the kids treat the gravity control like a glorified bungee jump, but no one watching them seemed concerned. Still, though, I had no inclinations to follow their lead.

It was only in the observatory that I found a bit of solace as I watched the stars and lost myself to the sweet incense of the tiny little fire-eater James gave me. The orange glob was the same texture as a slime, about the size of a plushie, and somewhat sentient. It moved on its own, preferred to be close to the soft heat of my body rather than near the cold display panels covering the dome, and I found it quite adorable. Whether it was some kind of technology or an animal from some foreign planet, I didn't know. What I did know was that a single match could keep it satisfied for hours and James had delivered on his promise — I had a stockpile of them now and was more than happy to strike them up and hand them over. The hazy smoke the little slime gave off was enough to make me forget my thoughts — my pain.

I named it Glupin the Third.

It was a dumb name for a dumb glob, but I liked it. It made me laugh. And though joy of any kind felt like a betrayal of the highest order, I couldn't change it.

Glupin was on its fourth matchstick, and the stars on the other side of the display panel were all but gone behind the thick haze of intoxicating smoke when the remnants of an argument floated up to me. My thoughts were an incoherent mess, but I managed to step over to the open side of the platform and peer over the edge.

The engineer, Chise, was standing in the atrium of Sector 4 with her two bickering apprentices, Pia, the mechanic, and Sigurd, the shipwright. I wasn't the only one peeking over the edge to watch their argument either, so I felt no shame in getting comfortable to enjoy the show. I leaned my back against the wall and slid down until I was cross-legged on the floor, resting my elbow on my knee and my chin in my hand. Chise was a thick woman — from her braids to her hips, she was nothing but rolls and curves. The streak of pink woven into her black hair complimented the glittering pink sparkles that drifted down from the bottom of her hoverchair. It carried her between Pia, a girl of maybe fifteen in dark green overalls, and Sigurd, a cyborg with pulsing blue lights streaking across his rich brown skin and circling his joints.

The observatory was several floors above them, at the very top of the ship, and my senses were dulled from Glupin's smoke. But as their tempers flared higher, their words became clearer, and I was grateful for the little translator James had given me with Glupin's matches. It was a tiny silver earring that curved around the upper part of my ear and rested on the bone there. I usually took it off in the observatory since I was alone and it felt awkward to wear it, but it was perfect for translating the words of everyone on the ship into something I could understand.

"She's not fit to lead us!" Sigurd yelled.

"Shut up!" Pia screamed back. "You don't know what she's going through!"

"And you do?" Sigurd shot back.

"I know what it's like to lose someone I love and respect!"

"And I don't?" Sigurd asked, incredulous. "My captain was killed too!"

"But you're a machine!" Pia screamed, her voice cracking as she balled her fists. "You don't even have emotions!"

"Enough!" Chise yelled, her soft voice cutting through theirs as Sigurd staggered back from Pia. "Enough," she repeated. "Like it or not, the lady is our captain now," she said, turning to pin glares on both of them. "And disrespecting each other over it solves nothing."

"He started it," Pia huffed, crossing her arms.

"And I'm finishing it," Chise said, her voice thrumming with finality. "Separate and cool off. We have work tomorrow. And I ain't gone have this ship failing because you two can't work together. Am I clear?" When neither of her apprentices spoke, she slammed her fist against the armrest of her chair and enunciated her words. "Am I clear?"

Sigurd glowered at Pia but nodded his head anyway. "Yes, ma'am."

"Ma'am," Pia muttered, nodding her head.

That was the end of things.

Pia stood there watching Chise and Sigurd disappear, and her shoulders shook as she glared down at the ground. And I don't know if it was the smoke, my loneliness, boredom, pure exhaustion, or because she was wearing every emotion that had been plaguing me since James told me Xavier was a corpse rather than a man now, but I grabbed one of the pillow cushions and tossed it down to her on a whim. It landed at her feet and she jumped, looking upward. Our gazes met and I waved her up.

She picked up the pillow and made her way to the observatory. She returned the cushion and apologized for the noise. I waved her off and invited her to stay — feed a match to Glupin.

She did.

The silence left behind by the argument was eaten away by the little radio. Whenever I focused on it, it almost seemed to be making sense.

Almost.

But even with the translator, the sounds were gibberish to me. And before long, my fleeting thoughts were skittering away from me again. They were nothing worth chasing after, so I let them roam free. I had no desire to think about anything — to examine the emotions clinging to the inside of my brain or pick apart what they might mean. For the few moments I was engulfed in Glupin's smoke, I was free. And I was loath to give that up. So, Pia and I sat together in silence.

It wasn't until Glupin's haze was starting to disperse and she was reaching for another match that I dared to roll my head over to study her. She was oval-faced with big, violet eyes. Her lashes were thick and full, and her lips were shaped in the perfect pout. Her smooth brown skin reminded me of shiny russet potatoes — which was a weird thought to have, because who looks like potatoes? But before I could even think about where that thought had come from, I was struck by an insatiable craving for french fries — the thin, salty kind I used to pick up from a drive-thru window after a long day at work. I wondered if anyone in the cafeteria knew how to make them — would be willing to make them for me.

I was the captain, after all.

But just thinking those words made me want to laugh. Because, was I? James was the one running the ship. He was the one who set the destinations and handled the crew and made sure I ate something whenever I didn't appear in the dining hall — which was never. I hadn't stepped foot inside it since James gave me the grand tour on my first day. I could barely remember to feed myself, yet somehow, I was expected to be responsible for everyone else on the ship?

That was a joke.

The idea alone was hilarious, and with Glupin's smoke loosening my tongue and muddling my inhibitions, I couldn't contain my amusement. Snorts and chortles escaped from me until I was clutching my stomach.

"What's so funny?"

"I'm the captain of this ship," I forced out, wheezing at the words. Pia lifted her brows at me, and I mimicked her expression. "I'm the captain of this ship," I repeated, fully expecting her to get the joke if I just said the words again. "Me," I added, trying to stifle my giggles, "the grieving human woman who knows nothing about space. Isn't that just..."

I couldn't finish the sentence. I dissolved into another round of laughter and gave up on trying to restrain myself. What point was there in doing that? It felt almost sacrilegious to feel any kind of happiness, but this was the first time I'd felt anything other than pure and unadulterated misery since boarding the ship, and I wasn't ready to let go of this moment yet. I couldn't.

So I laughed.

Pia watched me and Glupin blew smoke into the air and the tiny radio kept singing in the background until reality fell away and we were nothing more than two unlikely souls — untethered and drifting through the stars together.

28 DAYS A WIDOW

"Do you ever miss the sun?"

The question caught me off guard and I worked to pry my heavy eyelids apart to look at Pia. She sat next to me, her head resting on the wall across from me as she watched the stars pass us by. Her legs faced the window panel, mine faced the tiny radio on the opposite side of the room. It hummed its tune incessantly, and the songs seemed sadder than usual. As if the radio heard all of our quiet emotions and returned them to us in sweet melodies.

"What?"

"The sun," Pia repeated. Glupin rested in her lap, squishing around her fingers as she idly pressed into it. It jiggled as if it was pleased, but I wasn't convinced it was fully sentient. Did slimes have emotions? I stared at the tiny blob for a moment, and it jiggled again, as if it could tell I was looking at it. But maybe I just imagined that part.

"Do you ever miss the sun?" Pia asked again.

"No."

That was an outright lie, but I didn't feel like finding the words to explain what I felt to her. My mind was too hazy. And stringing together words seemed like a job I wasn't getting paid to do.

My throat had been thick since I'd climbed the stairs to the observatory. I'd fed Glupin its first match of the day what felt like hours ago, but still — my thoughts raced, refusing to slow and fall into the sweet, merciful reprieve Glupin's smoke always offered me.

Part of me hoped I was having a panic attack — that would've been much easier to deal with rather than whatever thoughts were plaguing me, but my normal distractions were failing me. Suddenly, the pillows were too soft. The music too loud. The smoke too thick.

The stars too far away to offer me any light in this dark place.

And even with Pia sitting next to me, I couldn't help but feel trapped. Stuck in the void of space with nothing to do but choke on my own existence.

But I had no one to save me. Not anymore.

And that reminder made tears burn in the corners of my eyes, but I blinked them away. I refused to cry in front of a child, even if she was no happier than me. Besides, what good would tears do? They would only clog my already swollen throat, and how pathetic would it be to suffocate from my own misery? I refused to accept that future, so I pushed Pia's question, and every thought that came with it, away. Because there was no way for me to catch my breath.

It's not like I could step outside for some fresh air.

Or go for a drive.

Or find solace in the arms of my husband when he was decomposing in the ground.

There were too many things ripping gaping black holes into my life to simply ask if I missed the sun. Because of course I did — what human wouldn't?

The manufactured lights aboard the ship could never compare, no matter how hard Chise and Sigurd worked to imitate it. But there were things I missed more that made the sun's absence seem insignificant. Things that made my chest ache and my heart pound and my soul mourn a future that would never exist. Things that made me want to cry out in anguish every day I woke up and realized that I was still alive. Things that made me want to give up every time I was reminded that I'd have to continue living without them.

But who would understand that?

How could I explain that?

Every breath felt like a fight for my life. And it was a fight I desperately wanted to lose. It was almost a shame that the gravity control on the ship would keep me from plummeting to my death. Otherwise, I could just step over the edge. Go headfirst and let myself fall.

It would only be terrifying for a moment.

"Lady Kyra?"

Pia's soft voice pulled me back from my spiraling thoughts, and I let my eyes slide over to her.

"What?"

"What was Captain Zay like on Earth?"

Captain Zay.

I knew that's how most of the crew referred to him, but hearing it was still a knife twisting through my gut. That version of him was completely foreign to me.

"He was wonderful," I answered, my voice little more than a hoarse whisper. "Funny. Brilliant. Had a solution for every problem."

"You loved him?"

"Yes."

"He loved you, too," she said, her declaration brimming with absolute certainty. "More than the stars, I think. Cause we never stayed on a planet so long before. At least," she shrugged and offered me a sheepish smile, "that's what I've heard from Chise and Sigurd. I was left with the crew a few days after I was born. So, Star Prime 1307 is the only planet I've really spent any real time on. We never went too far from your solar system. Never more than seven cycles away."

"Oh, yeah?"

"Yep. Captain Zay never wanted to be too far from you," Pia answered, her eyes drifting closed as she took in a deep breath. "Some of the people on the attack squad were bored. Mad that we never got to fight anymore. But most everybody was happy for Captain Zay. Especially Sigurd. He was glad the captain was happy." She paused and nodded with a sleepy smile on her lips. "I was too."

"Were you close to him?"

"To Sigurd? He's like a brother, I guess," she said, scrunching up her face. "An annoying one."

I smiled at that. "I meant Xavier," I clarified. "Were you close to him?"

I didn't really want to know the answer to this question — I didn't want to know the secrets he'd never be able to tell me now. But I didn't want to not know either. I craved her answer, and my heart boxed against the inside of my ribs like a wild animal trying to break free as I waited.

"Kinda. I admired him," she whispered, her voice cracking as she turned her head away from me. "Everyone did. And he really looked out for all of us. Saved us. Saved me," she said, sucking down a shuddering breath. "I miss him."

I almost cracked at those words. The carefully built wall around my emotions almost gave way. Almost crumbled beneath the weight of her grief and mine.

I didn't understand my own thoughts and emotions right now, so there was no way I'd be able to decipher those of a fifteen-year-old girl when she was mourning a captain I'd never met. Even if her captain was the husband I'd buried, we weren't mourning the same person. Even if our feelings looked similar, we weren't the same.

Mourning a lover and a savior couldn't be compared.

So, I didn't try to.

Instead, I sat up and reached for Glupin, lifted it into my lap, and fed it another match. It hummed and glubbed before spewing out its hazy smoke. Today, it smelled of morning dew and lemonade and it made me sick for the tiny blue planet I'd left behind.

I took a deep breath of it before daring to glance at Pia again. Tears streaked down her round cheeks, and I blinked back every emotion that threatened to break free of my carefully built dam — threatened to drown me beneath waves of thoughts and feelings I never wanted.

But I wasn't a child. My walls wouldn't fall as easily as hers did. Still, I nudged her foot with mine so she wouldn't forget that she wasn't alone.

"Yeah," I whispered, nodding when she looked up at me. "I miss him too."

40 (?) DAYS A WIDOW

There was no day and night cycle among the stars. I could only guess at how much time passed by how often I slept. Which was a lot. Probably more than I should have. But there wasn't much to do on *The Reveler* aside from eat, sleep, and smoke.

I woke up alone.

I ate alone.

I slept alone.

The only time I had company that could talk back to me was when Pia joined me in the observatory. She came by whenever she could. And I learned more about the ship and the crew from her than I ever did from James or Xavier. Probably because Pia volunteered information while those two had only ever answered my sparse questions.

Everyone on the ship had a role, but this crew was more than just business. It was a family and my heart trembled whenever I thought about just how much Xavier had left out of his stories.

He'd always been more than happy to regale with me with his adventures. Tales of beating back dock bandits with metal pipes, hunting down wanted captains for the KUAF — the Known Universe's Allied Federation — and rescuing the family members that his crew had to leave behind when they joined him. Xavier had never been short of a story. So, I'd thought I'd had an inkling of what his world — his other life — was like. But his stories always centered around himself and James and the epic fights they fought.

I'd never even known the names of most of the crew — hadn't realized how many of them there were.

And I'd never believed Xavier to be a perfect man, but it was a unique kind of torture to learn new sides of him from a stranger. And it made me sad in ways I had no words for. I would never know Pia's version of the man I loved — of Captain Zay — except through the fading memories of other people. And with every word she spoke, what remained of my spirit shattered into indecipherable pieces.

But I listened regardless.

I let her grieve the captain she'd lost, just as she let me grieve the husband I'd buried.

We hurt together.

And somewhere in that haze, we found comfort.

"How did you meet Captain Zay, Lady Kyra?"

One of the things I learned about Pia early on was that she liked to ask questions. She was more than content to sit in the quiet hum of the radio and Glupin's glubbing as it munched on the first match she gave it, but by the second one her violet eyes were glued to the stars and her thoughts were lost to places I'd never been.

Sometimes she asked me about Earth. Most of the time, she asked me about Xavier. What he'd been like — larger than life. Or what stories he'd told me — all of the ones where he'd been the valiant hero. What foods he'd liked on Earth — fried chicken wings and honey-butter yeast rolls. Those were easy things to answer. But this time… this question felt personal.

Too personal.

But the story was spilling out of me before I could stop it. Begging for someone — anyone — to hear it.

"Before I met Xavier, I was a teacher," I answered, striking another match and passing it over to Glupin, watching as it bobbed up and down before hissing out a stream of smoke that smelled of copy paper, drip coffee, cardboard pizza and sweaty children bathed in pungent body spray. At some point, I'd realized that Glupin smelled like whatever memory was the strongest in my mind. I would probably never understand how it worked, but I loved that it did. It brought me back to moments I'd forgotten about. Brought me back to Xavier, if only for a moment. "He wandered into the school one day, looking for directions. I'm the one who gave them to him."

"Is that all?"

"That's all," I said, taking a deep breath of Glupin's smoke and leaning back against the wall and letting my eyes trail over the stars. "I wish I had a more interesting story to tell you." The corners of my mouth twitched at the memory. "I just happened to be in the front office making copies when he walked in. Because the one on my hall was broken, as usual," I added.

"What was wrong with it?"

"Who knows?" I shrugged. "Out of paper. Out of ink. Out of toner. Whatever it was, I was up front that day. And I'm glad I was."

"Where was Captain Zay going?"

"The public library," I answered, smirking. "He was always lost without James telling him where to go. And his misguided sense of direction brought him to my school instead."

"He always did love books," Pia whispered.

"More like he wanted to see if his adventures ever made it into one," I chuckled. "He had an ego bigger than the galaxy itself. But he loved a good story," I whispered, my throat feeling thick. "Always looking for his next great adventure."

"Did you go with him?" Pia asked. "To the library, I mean."

"No," I laughed. "I was working. But he did come back the next day," I said, smiling at the memory. The secretary, Jillian, had called my classroom from the front desk, asking if I knew a bald man dressed in all black and if I wanted her to call the police. I'd told her to hold off on doing that, knowing I'd never sleep right again if I encouraged a white woman to call the police on a Black man simply for needing directions.

And curiosity had its claws in me.

The grin that had split his face when I'd stepped into the office was enough to make me do a double take. I hadn't paid much attention to him the day before, but now I let my eyes linger on him — crawl over his dimpled face and dark eyes to his broad shoulders and muscled legs clad in dark wash jeans and heavy boots. The man was the very definition of the word handsome, and I was intrigued. I was grateful to have worn my houndstooth pants with my red sweater, block-heeled pumps, and lipstick — my favorite work outfit. It was like armor and filled me with a fresh wave of reckless confidence when he'd asked for my name and to meet me after school.

I was a fool to say yes to a stranger, but I would've been a bigger one had I said no. We met for coffee a few days later. And one moment turned to twelve years in the blink of an eye.

"And that's when you found out he was an alien?"

"Absolutely not," I said, laughing again. "I didn't find that out until months later," I admitted. "He would sometimes disappear for a week or two at a time, but I didn't really notice in the beginning. Once we started officially dating though, it was obvious. He said he worked in transport, so I figured he was just a truck driver or something," I sighed and tugged at the ends of my afro. "I had no idea he was an alien. It wasn't until we got into a pretty heated discussion about him ignoring my calls whenever he was gone that he finally told me the truth."

"And you believed him?"

"I broke up with him," I said, shrugging when Pia's mouth fell open in shock. "Who would believe the guy they were dating was an alien? It's not like he was walking around with green skin and bug eyes. It would've made more sense if he was just cheating on me."

"Captain Zay would've never done that," Pia said, shaking her head definitively. "Never."

"Yeah, well," I sighed. "It's not like there were a bunch of aliens on Earth to corroborate his story."

"True," Pia agreed, nodding. "Star Prime 1307 was kinda primitive. You guys didn't even have a proper dock for the ship." She glanced over to me and offered a slight shrug. "No offense."

"None taken."

"How did Captain Zay convince you he was telling the truth?"

"He didn't. I mean, he tried to, but in a situation like that, everything sounds like a lie. It was James who convinced me."

"Really?"

I nodded.

"He caught me after a movie on my day off. I'd met him once before, so I was a bit suspicious because, of course, he only confirmed everything Xavier had told me. But James was his best friend, so why wouldn't he, you know?" I scoffed and shook my head, smiling at the memory. "It wasn't until James pulled out a…" I snapped my fingers and frowned, "carspiculas? The purple flower that talks?"

"Carspendilas," Pia corrected. "They're from a tiny planet in the Pursinian Galaxy. Carson grows them downstairs in Sector 5."

"James brought me some. They sang me a song and begged me to believe their captain. So, naturally, I screamed and ran away," I laughed. "But when Xavier came back around to plead his case, I heard him out."

"And then you believed him?"

"And then I believed him," I said, nodding. "It took some adjusting, but it's not like I was having much luck or fun dating Earth men," I said, rolling my eyes at the memory. "And meeting Zay was the best thing that ever happened to me. I wasn't going to just throw that away when he was telling me the truth."

"You know," Pia hummed, giggling behind her hand as I finished telling her our story. "I think you were the most normal part of Captain Zay's life."

I was about to feel all types of offended at her words. It felt like she was calling me boring — like I'd been the ball and chain that held Xavier back from the stars he loved. And that would've been a misery I just wouldn't have been able to bear. But then she spoke again.

"I'm glad he had you," she whispered. "He would seem so distant sometimes, you know? Like he was somewhere else completely. And I always wondered what was going on in his head. What great adventure he was planning next. But," she paused and sighed, tilting her head to face me, "maybe he was just thinking about you."

"Maybe."

"Probably," Pia said, nodding. "Everyone wants to go home when they're away from it. And as much as we wanted to be that for him," she said, turning back to face the stars, her voice sounding wet, "I think you were home for him, Lady Kyra. And I, at least, will always be extremely grateful to you for that." She threw a weak smile in my direction. "Thank you for giving our wandering captain a home to go back to."

57 (?) DAYS A WIDOW

I left my room without Glupin for the first time since James gifted it to me.

I fed it a match and left it floating in the hot water of my bathtub. It liked to float there for hours, and maintaining the temperature of the water was nothing more than a push of a button. But it would likely be days before Pia found time to see me again.

Sigurd had come to the observatory yesterday and yelled at her for slacking off — something about needing her and the mechanic team to aid his shipwrights in reconfiguring the water transport lines between Sectors 6 and 7.

I'd asked her once what the difference between her job as a mechanic and Sigurd's was, and after throwing me the most insulted look I'd ever seen, she explained that while he and his team of shipwrights worked to fix and maintain the ship itself, her team of mechanics managed the technology onboard. They sounded like the same thing to me, but she assured me they were not. And though she complained the whole time Sigurd was dragging her back to work, she made her apologies to me and followed behind him anyway, throwing snippy remarks at his back as they jumped over the open ledge of the observatory and disappeared down the hallway in Sector 9. I'd known she was a mechanic and Chise's apprentice, but it wasn't until Sigurd was basically dragging her back to Sector 10 that it occurred to me that she had a job on the ship. It was an uncomfortable experience to realize a child was doing more than I was, and something about her extended absence nudged a quiet part of mind — pressed a hand to my back as I walked the pristine white halls of *The Reveler.*

It felt both antiseptic and homey. The tile was a gleaming white and the bright lights threatened me with a migraine, but it was welcoming in a way I hadn't noticed when James had guided me through the pseudo-city of the ship.

Pictures of different worlds lined the halls and there was a constant chatter drifting from the center of the ship. There were nine main floors inside *The Reveler,* broken up into overlapping sectors.

The control center sat like an onyx sphere overlooking it all from Sector 3. Sectors 4 through 8 were where most of the people were. They roamed about, dipping into shops, watering plants, running businesses, and raising families. My mind stuttered every time I saw it, but Xavier had told me once that *The Reveler* was more than just a transport vessel — it was home to hundreds of creatures. I'd always assumed he'd been exaggerating — being generous with his words to impress the naïve human woman he loved — but it was easy to understand why he'd said *The Reveler* was like its own little micro-planet, drifting through the galaxies.

I thought about how Pia had never known anything other than the ship and looked at the kids running around on Sector 8. It wouldn't have surprised me at all to know there were some who'd been born on the ship — knew no other home than the one called *The Reveler*. Had known no other leader than the one named Captain Zay. Tears burned the corners of my eyes at the thought as I stood by the railing on the fourth level and witnessed the true scale of the ship. Seeing everyone onboard push forward with their lives as we sailed through the galaxies was an experience like nothing else.

Both awe-inspiring and humbling.

Xavier had built an incredible home for so many and still had chosen to stay with me. It was a subtle reminder that we were all nothing more than insignificant dots, just floating through the universe in the same direction until someone chooses to notice us. And Xavier had noticed me.

He'd been the sun of his own solar system and still chose to shine light into my world. And now, everything felt darker without him. The weight of his absence crushed my lungs, and my throat felt tight as I pushed away from the railing, unsure of where I was going — just knowing that I was going somewhere.

There were tiny globs like Glupin roaming the halls, munching on dust and debris, keeping the floors and walls and display panels clean. They were varying shades of teal and silver, and part of me wanted to name each one as I passed by, but I knew there was no real point to that.

I'd never be able to tell them apart. I was too disoriented to even tell up from down — I just knew that I had to keep moving.

Because if I stopped, I'd break.

So I found myself navigating the shifting lines of pipework and pulsating grids of Sector 10. It was basically the outer shell of the ship, and I'd stumbled through one of the myriad of hidden doors scattered throughout the different sectors. I'd wandered for what felt like hours before I stepped into the engineering workroom. There were three desks set up in the space — two with thick black chairs in front of them. The last, I guessed, was for Chise since she had her own hoverchair, but each desk was littered with designs and tools I had no names for. My heart lifted for a brief moment at the passing thought I might run into Pia, but it was Sigurd I saw instead.

He stood in the center of a revolving image of the ship, zooming in on some component I'd never understand. I held my breath, watching as his cybernetic eyes traced over the designs and his fingers — still made of flesh and blood — sketched something across a rectangular display in his hand. My mind could only understand it as a tablet, but it seemed like it would shatter into flecks of light rather than glass if he were to drop it. He hummed a soft melody under his breath as he worked, but when his attention found me, he froze and the room fell silent.

He stepped out of the neon pink light detailing the ship and it blinked out of existence as he crossed his arms, narrowing his gaze at me.

"Did you need something?"

"Just exploring," I said. "I didn't realize the ship was so complex."

"Because coasting at light speed is easy," he said, his eyes whirring as he rolled them.

"Did I imply that it was?" I asked, holding his dark blue gaze. He stared back at me, his full lips set in an unamused line as he glared at me.

"What is it that you want?" Sigurd asked, letting out a slow breath.

"Do I need to need something?" I shot back, finding slight amusement in the way his jaw clenched at my constant questions. It was too easy to get under his skin and the argument I'd overheard between him and Pia all those weeks ago began to make less and less sense to me. Pia had accused him of being heartless when it was clear that Sigurd had emotions.

He tried far too hard to hide them all.

"Most people don't come wandering around the mechanic room unless they want something," he clarified. "And Pia isn't here."

"I wasn't looking for her," I said, letting my gaze dart around the room before finally admitting, "I just got a little lost."

"There is a map on the wall every five-hundred paces," Sigurd said, dropping his arms. "And the teal slimes can lead you anywhere."

"Oh," I whispered, my eyes growing wide as I thought back to all the globs I'd passed on my way here. "I didn't know that."

"Probably because you didn't want to know."

"That's rude," I said, narrowing my gaze at him.

"Is it not true?" he countered, lifting a dark brow at me. "I doubt James would've let you roam the ship without telling you how to get around. He's not that kind of thoughtless man." He shrugged and turned back to the pink display of the ship that returned to its full size at the flick of his fingers. "But I wouldn't be surprised if you were the kind of thoughtless woman who wouldn't give him your attention."

I had no words for that. It felt like a slight that went much deeper than my getting lost on the ship. But as much as I hated to admit it, I couldn't say that I'd retained much about James's tour. Other than the control center, my room, the Captain's Quarters, the observatory, and the exit, I had no idea where anything was. Everything about my first day aboard the ship was like static in my memory — fuzzy, silent, and unfocused. I knew James had given me plenty of information about how the ship worked, but I'd be lying if I said I could recall any of it.

I hadn't been in the best headspace that day, but having Sigurd point out that my ignorance was my own fault made my face burn and my anger spark to life. It was safer than feeling guilt or embarrassment or shame.

Anger was safe. So, I clung to it.

"Is it okay for you to talk down to me like that?" I questioned, drawing his attention back to me. "I am technically the captain of this ship, you know?"

The title felt sticky and awkward in my mouth. It wasn't mine to lay claim to. Not really. Not when this whole conversation was only happening because I was getting lost on the ship. Not when I was throwing the title around just to prove I belonged when we both knew I didn't.

I didn't belong anywhere anymore.

But I refused to take the words back. Even if they made my skin crawl and tasted bitter in my mouth, they were true. This was my husband's ship. Xavier left it to me. I was the captain now. And this ship had a hierarchy — that much I knew.

And Sigurd knew that I knew that he knew that too.

"Then act like it, *Lady Kyra*," he hissed, the screws in his jaw twisting as his blue eyes narrowed to slits. "Or give the title to someone who wants it."

"Someone like you?"

"I have work to do," he snapped, turning his back to me. "So, if there's nothing else, you can leave out the same way you came in, *Captain.*"

He seethed as I stood there, and it was easy to imagine a trail of steam spewing from his ears like the cartoons my dad had loved to watch on the weekends. It was almost funny. But it reminded me of Glupin and I suddenly ached for the sweet smell it put off — wondered if it would smell of pancakes and bacon and freshly cut grass. My throat felt dry just thinking about it, so I left Sigurd to his work and returned to my room.

It was easy enough to find with a map.

68 (?) DAYS A WIDOW

We landed on a planet I couldn't pronounce, and I had no idea what galaxy we were in, though I was sure James had told me at least twice.

My thoughts were getting hazier by the day, and somehow, that didn't bother me. With each passing day I cared less and less that I was deteriorating, morphing from a woman into a leech — relying solely on James to keep me alive and waiting for the day he gave up on me and let me rot in peace.

I spent my morning in the bath with Glupin, soaking until my brown skin turned to prunes. And when I got out, I could do nothing more than smile at James as he updated me on *The Reveler*. I tried to listen to him — I really did — but I was mostly waiting for him to be done. I knew nothing of the mechanics of the ship. I knew nothing of the stars we sailed through, the people who traveled with us, or the destinations we were trying to reach.

My mind was empty.

Blank.

Full of the sweet thoughts Glupin fed me, and I missed the little blob whenever we were apart. I started imagining its squishy form and checked out of the conversation with James completely.

He asked if I was okay.

I told him not to worry about me.

He warned me to slow down on how much time I spent with Glupin.

I told him to mind his own business.

He told me that I am his business, and I laughed in his face.

"I'm a widow," I snapped at him. "I'm no one's business anymore."

He opened his mouth to say something else, but I left him standing there. I wasn't getting off the ship. I wasn't talking to aliens. I wasn't exploring a new planet.

I refused to experience anything Xavier should've shown me himself.

I didn't want any new memories Xavier wouldn't share with me.

James called after me, but I ignored him.

I sank into my bed.

I fed Glupin a match.

And in the silence of the empty ship, I slept.

93 (?) DAYS A WIDOW

I didn't leave *The Reveler* a single time while we were in the Pursinian Galaxy. Pia told me that's where we were — Ireshia, the second in a string of planets rumored to be one of the most beautiful in the Known Universe.

But I didn't leave my room — not even for the observatory. It felt too much like work to force myself out of bed. To get dressed. To be perceived by anyone.

I hadn't taken a breath of fresh air since my argument with James. I hadn't laid eyes on him. And he hadn't given me any matches since then, either. It felt like some kind of odd war of attrition, but Pia proved herself a reliable aid.

It was only when she stopped by to bring me food and a new supply of matches that I realized time had passed.

She told me of the outside world — of Chise and James and Sigurd and the triplets and the engines that powered the ship and the crew. And it was only when she grew silent that I heard her unspoken words.

She hadn't left the ship either.

And that made my already slow thoughts stop.

Pia was fifteen.

Her world should be bigger than mine.

She should know more than *The Reveler* when the entire Known Universe was at her fingertips. But when I tried to question her, my tongue was too thick to move and my thoughts had moseyed on farther than I could grasp. So, instead, I sighed and sunk deeper into the bed, burying myself beneath the heap of blankets.

"You should go outside."

Those were the only words I could muster.

"There's nothing out there for me," she hummed, leaning her head back against the wall. She sat cross-legged on the floor by the door, and she looked as small as I felt. "Captain Zay was the only one who cared about me. So, what's the point of seeing the universe without him?"

What indeed…

94 (?) DAYS A WIDOW

Pia left my door cracked.

It wasn't a big deal since no one ever walked past my room. It was too far away — the last room on a dead end hallway. And no one would dare harm the captain's wife. But the thick orange haze of smoke had faded, seeping through the tiny space Pia had left behind. And even the slightest bit of clarity felt like an assault on my senses.

I hated it.

Glupin bobbed on the floor next to my bed, stretching and expanding as it did whenever it was cold, and I reached for another match. But in the darkness, I saw Xavier.

Tall and handsome as he always was, his arms were crossed across his broad chest and his black eyes were trained on me. He didn't smile, though.

And Xavier was always smiling.

Instead, he shook his head.

"Aren't you done yet, Ky?"

"You don't get to tell me how to grieve you," I whispered, my voice hoarse and my eyes blurry and my chest burning and my anger raging and my muscles twitching. I couldn't tell if it was from the weight of everything I was feeling or my dwindling high or the fact it was the middle of Ireshia's night and I was still half-asleep, but I couldn't move. I could only stare at Xavier from across the room.

"But aren't you done yet?" he asked again.

"If you want me to be done, then stop me."

"Stop yourself," he said. "Or don't. Not like I could ever change your mind."

"What do you care?" I asked, tears flowing freely down my face as I glared at him. "You're dead. You died, and you left me here!" I screamed. And part of me heard the shuffling outside my door, but I didn't care how crazy I would look if someone found me now. I couldn't stop the flood of emotions — of words. The feelings I'd spent the past few months running from were staring me down and refusing to let me look away.

"You were supposed to outlive me by a thousand years and yet…" I sobbed. "You're gone! And I'm here. And what am I supposed to do?" I asked, my voice cracking as I tried to blink away the tears to see him clearly. "This was supposed to be *our* adventure," I said, finding the strength to swing my legs over the side of the bed and glare at him.

"Then why didn't you ever come with me, Ky?"

"What?" The word was strangled as it fell out of my mouth, weighed down by all the guilt that had been suffocating me for months.

"You know why…"

"Do I?" he asked. "You're screaming at me for not being here to take you on this adventure, but you never came with me," he said. "And I begged you to come with me, Ky. Every time. But you never said yes."

"Because I had dreams," I said, shaking my head and scrambling for words. "Plans. I couldn't just leave everything behind, not knowing if we'd ever come back. I had things I wanted to do, Zay."

"Everything was always more important to you than I was."

"No!" I screamed, clenching my fists in my sheets and fighting for the strength to break free from whatever was pinning my body to the bed. "Nothing was more important than you. Not to me," I sobbed. "But you were supposed to live forever. I only had a few decades. You were everything to me, but…" I shook my head and dug the heels of my palms into my eyes, "we were supposed to have more time."

"I wish you had said yes," he whispered. "Just once."

"I'm saying it now," I sobbed, reaching out for him, desperate to grab hold of him for just a moment. "I'm saying yes now! But you're not here. You tapped out before we ever got started. You just up and died!"

"But you didn't die with me," he said.

I sucked in a sharp breath at his words. They were both sad and defiant, and they stirred some long dormant emotion in my chest that burned as if metal claws were tearing at my heart. I bit my trembling bottom lip, but I didn't know what I could say in the wake of such a resounding statement.

"If you want to die, Ky, then have James turn the ship around and climb into the grave next to me," he said, shrugging. "But you're not going to do that.”

“You don’t know that,” I whispered, my voice trembling so much that not even I believed my bluff.

“I do,” he said, offering me a weak smile. “Because I know my wife. If she wanted to do something, it would have already been done.”

“Your wife is a widow,” I said, my voice little more than a whisper in the dark.

“Yes,” Xavier said. “Because she’s still alive. And I want her to keep living.”

“Without you?”

“It never stopped you before,” he said, his face fading in the dark.

“Don’t go!” I shouted, springing up from the bed as if I’d been released from the devil’s grasp. I tried to move closer, but my feet got tangled in the fallen sheets. I stepped on Glupin instead and it squished under my foot — soft and warm like the slime it resembled. But I didn’t let my thoughts linger on it.

Xavier was fading away, and I desperately wanted to keep him with me for as long as I could. Even a second longer would be enough.

“I love you, Ky,” he said, smiling at me. “Go have your adventures.”

And then he was gone — quick as he came. And I couldn’t stop the wail that broke free from me. The shuffling outside my door returned and before I could collapse to the ground, James was catching me — hauling me into his chest and holding me upright as I wept and screamed and slammed my fists against him. I heard his words of comfort, but they might as well have been gibberish to me.

I didn’t need them.

What I needed was to stand my ground against the feelings of anger and betrayal I had been running from. I had to look at Xavier's memory and hold space for all the ragged edges it left me with. I would acknowledge the gaping hole in my life he left behind and I would drag myself out from the depths of despair and self-loathing I'd been wallowing in.

Tonight, I would weep for the past.

Tomorrow, I would stare down the future.

95 DAYS A WIDOW

The first thing I did after prying myself from bed was return Glupin to James. He accepted it without a word and neither one of us spoke of that night again.

103 DAYS A WIDOW

I spent a week in the infirmary throwing up orange gunk. Turns out, Glupin wasn't as harmless as I'd thought it was. Its smoke was parasitic and for the past ninety-some-odd days, it'd been making a cozy home in my body. In small doses, it was fine. Harmless. Good even, according to Venra, the doctor onboard.

I didn't really understand her explanation, but the parasites were benign. Symbiotic. They lived in the lungs and were the reason any of us could survive in space.

It's probably why James had given it to me.

But in large doses, Glupin caused hallucinations.

Then seizures.

Then death.

"Why didn't you tell me this would happen?"

I'd asked the question when James had come to visit me. It was during one of the rare times I wasn't heaving into a bucket and could form coherent sentences.

"I did."

"No, you didn't."

"I did."

"When?"

"When I gave it to you."

"Liar."

"You just didn't listen," he said, holding back my afro and ignoring the orange chunks that landed on his shoes as I shoved my face into the bucket again.

I couldn't argue with that logic, even if I'd wanted to. I didn't remember much about anything after the funeral. And it's not like he'd forced me to keep feeding Glupin matches. It was my own fault for not listening to his warnings. And for ignoring him when he'd tried to get me to slow down. And for asking Pia to bring me matches when he'd cut off my supply.

And it's not like I would've just let him take Glupin back.

This was the bed I made for myself. I'd have to lie in it.

And maybe James had had his reasons. Maybe he'd known this was how things would turn out — that I'd spiral out of control until I caught myself. He'd be a truly wise man if he did.

Or a fool.

I started puking up more gunk before I could remind myself to figure out which one he was.

113 DAYS A WIDOW

Once Venra released me, I took some time to actually explore the vessel I'd be calling home for the foreseeable future. With a sober mind, I could appreciate the craftmanship of *The Reveler*. There was always a display panel or dome to see into the void of space, no matter where you found yourself. It kept *The Reveler* from feeling claustrophobic and I trailed my fingers along the cool walls as I walked the halls, committing the pathways to memory.

It didn't take me long to end up at the observatory.

I was empty-handed, and still my breath was taken away from me.

"Beautiful, isn't it?"

I tore my gaze away from the myriad of stars floating by to look at James. He lounged against the cushions in the center of the bench, his long legs stretched out in front of him as he stared out at the stars. I'd spent most of my days up here — either peering at the stars or over the edge at the people down below. Now, I fell onto the dark blue cushions beside James and stared out at the void we coasted through.

"Why didn't Xavier leave this ship to you?" I asked. "Doesn't the first mate take over in the absence of the captain?"

"He loved you more than me."

"No, he didn't," I said, snorting. "Differently, sure," I added. "But not more."

After a silence that stretched out so long I'd nearly forgotten our conversation, James sighed.

"You want my theory?"

"Wouldn't have asked if I didn't," I said.

"I think he wanted us to see the stars together." James let out a deep, unsteady breath, and I was reminded that his world had imploded the same day mine had. "What better way to make sure I took you to space than to leave you the ship?"

The words took up all the air in the observatory and my chest burned as they sunk into my skin. Salty tears pooled in the corners of my eyes, and this time I held nothing back as they spilled over and raced down my face.

"He would think something like that," I said, letting a lone bark of laughter escape me. "He always wanted us to be friends."

"I always thought we were."

"Me too," I agreed, swiping at my eyes. "Thanks for bringing me along."

"I wouldn't have left you behind," James said, shrugging. "He made me promise to look after you if anything ever happened to him. I never thought..." his words trailed off as he shook his head and cleared his throat. "No matter what happens, Ky, I've got your back. Always."

"Thanks, Jay," I said, using the nickname Xavier had given him when they were kids. James's face softened at the sound of it and the ice in my heart melted a bit knowing I had someone in my corner I could trust. "And for what it's worth," I said, knocking my boot against his, "I've got yours too."

We sat in comfortable silence for a while, consumed by our own thoughts. I thought of all the possibilities that lay before us now, and the tiniest of smiles slipped across my lips as I watched the brilliant lights of the universe slip by us.

"I guess we belong to the stars now, huh?"

"We revel among them," James said.

"Is that why…"

"Now you're getting it, Ky," James said, grinning. "Now you're getting it."

115 DAYS
A WIDOW

It was only after I had explored the rest of the ship that I dared to venture back into the control center. The triplets let their eyes linger on me, but James was the only one who acknowledged my presence by calling out that the captain was at the helm. It made me feel very much like a pirate, and I couldn't help the sparks of excitement that danced across my skin and up my arms.

"Where are we going?" I asked, walking over to where James sat in the center of the room. He was seated at the center console, just to the right of the empty seat in the middle. It was clear the final seat was meant for the captain, but I moved to stand behind James rather than sit in what felt like a trap. The triplets let their gazes return to their work, but their eavesdropping wasn't subtle.

"Where would you like to go?"

The question seemed big.

We were being consumed by the vastness of space, and there were countless planets and worlds I'd never seen. But the look in James' eyes told me he would take me wherever I wanted to go — no matter how crazy my request might seem. That was both reassuring and suffocating, because where did I want to go? Something in my spirit was soothed at knowing James would keep his word — that he wouldn't abandon me — but carrying the responsibility of the future was still too heavy for me.

That question seemed too important for someone like me to answer.

But then Xavier crossed my mind. I glanced over to what was no doubt his empty seat and a cold rage seeped into my blood. My fingers tightened on the back of James' chair and, like a switch had been flipped in my brain, every trace of hesitation I felt was gone.

"Do you know where he is?"

The question hung in the air, turning it rancid the longer it lingered. James, who had only let his eyes slide over to me earlier, turned his entire body to face me. I didn't have the stomach to speak the man's name, but the quiet fury in my words left no room to mistake my intentions.

"I have an inkling," James admitted.

"Take us there, then," I said, glaring out into the sea of planets we approached. "We finish Xavier's business before we do anything else."

"Are you prepared to do that?"

"I will be," I said, nodding.

"This is an order, then?" he asked, lifting his dark brows at me.

"Sure."

"We need the captain to be absolute," one of the triplets said, cutting their hazel eyes over to me. "If we're changing course, that is."

I glanced over and held her gaze. Whether she was Karmen, Keelah, or Kavira, I couldn't tell. But she had straight silver hair brushing her shoulders, pale blue skin like moonlight, bright hazel eyes, and two silver antennae sprouting three inches out of her forehead. Had she not turned around, I would've never noticed, and I reminded myself that Xavier had traversed most of the Known Universe — I was likely the only human on the ship. So, it would be crazy to cling to my version of normalcy. Everything I understood about the world — about the universe — would have to change, and this moment would be one of many that led me down a different path — one completely detached from the one I'd walked my entire life until now.

So, I nodded at her.

"We're changing course."

I filled the words with a confidence I didn't feel, and it felt odd to be giving orders to strangers. It reminded me of the first day I'd stepped foot into a classroom — too young and naïve to realize what it meant to be responsible for the future of another. Just desperate to make sure that every student had a fair chance at a bright future — had the tools to reach the stars they were told to aim for. But that seemed like a dozen lifetimes ago now, and this wouldn't be the first time I was left in charge with no idea of what I was doing.

I doubted it would be the last.

The woman holding my gaze smirked and nodded before turning back to her console as James stared at me, his black eyes sparkling like Xavier's had whenever something intrigued him. They were so much like brothers, I often forgot they never shared blood. It made me ache for the man who had called me his wife, but this moment wasn't one for sorrow.

I was being watched — judged — and I understood that. The triplets were the guides of this ship, in more ways than one. If they didn't acknowledge me, no one would. And they wanted a leader who would stand in front of them and guide the way — not a broken woman they had to drag along behind them. So, I stood firm in my orders and met their burning gazes, daring any of them to challenge me.

"Captain's orders heard?" James barked out, his tone taking on an edge I'd never heard from him before.

"Captain's orders heard!" The triplets replied in unison, pressing, tapping, and swiping on their screens until *The Reveler* tilted in a new direction.

"It takes about forty-five cycles to get to Zaigera if we don't take the hyperway," James said, turning to look at me, and I nodded in understanding.

"I'll be ready."

35 CYCLES TO ZAIGERA

I became aware of two things over the next ten days, following my first order.

The first was that I'd been little more than a ghost, haunting the ship in a haze of Glupin's smoke. James and Pia had been the only ones to speak to me, and I'd accepted that as normal. But my perception of things shifted once my head was clear. The ship was bigger than just those two people, and I had been a fool, choosing to be blind and ignorant to the lives taking shape around me.

I'd walked around, accepting hate and disappointment from people who'd offered me none. I'd misconstrued concern for condemnation — curiosity for callous judgment. But those were things I'd dressed myself in — had picked up and worn them like a patchwork jacket that never belonged to me and would never fit. Once I'd cast them off, that's when I noticed the crew. Noticed they weren't avoiding my eyes but nodding their heads in respect.

It was a far cry from being ignored.

And there was a specific brand of shame that tried to cling to me, but I brushed it aside. I wouldn't apologize for my grief and the way it colored my world — the way it continued to shape it.

The way it continued to shape me.

But I wasn't ignorant. I could sense the anticipation on the ship. Like a palpable sheen settling along the walls and across our skins, I wasn't the only one getting ready for what was to come. And that's when I realized the truth.

They'd all been waiting for me to give the order to head to Zaigera.

Because James never would have. No matter how much he would've wanted to. Because that's not what Xavier would've wanted for me. Even I knew that much.

Xavier never wanted me to be anything but happy — to experience love and peace and joy in abundance. He'd wanted me to live a life filled with soft and beautiful things. Deep breath moments. Delicious foods, warm hugs, incredible music, and unexpected conversations. Laughter and pleasure. Tiny smiles, stolen looks, long naps, and the freedom to be — to exist exactly as I was without judgement, knowing I was seen and loved all the more because I was present. I was alive. And I was his.

He wouldn't want me chasing down a murderer, even if it was his own.

But Xavier didn't always get what he wanted in life — I wasn't going to start spoiling him now, in death. So, despite what we both knew his wishes to be, I gave the order and James followed it.

The Reveler wasn't the same place after that.

But the biggest change was that Pia no longer came around.

I was busier now. I could admit that.

Time was relative in space — more a social construct than any real unit of measure, but still. We would reach Zaigera eventually. And there was no time to waste if I wanted to be prepared for what awaited us there.

I couldn't spend all my time in the observatory like I used to.

I was forced to split my time between the control room, where James taught me the controls of the ship and how to read maps of the Known Universe; the infirmary, where Venra injected my muscles with microbiotics that strengthened my body and implanted new memories into them so that I could fight; and the training deck, where Sigurd, of all people, trained me in combat.

He was a confusing man, to say the least of him. He hadn't been shy about his disdain for me, but he'd been the first crew member to volunteer his help. James hadn't been surprised, though. Sigurd, aside from being Chise's first apprentice, was also the head of defense for *The Reveler*. With the exception of James — and Xavier, when he'd been alive — Sigurd was the best fighter aboard the ship. He was both sword and shield, defending the ship from all enemies and dispatching them when needed.

I'd been hesitant to trust him the first time James had left us alone in the training hall — which was more of an expansive dome than a hall — but I'd learned to give up all my expectations when it came to being in space. Nothing was as it seemed.

Not the ship.

Not the crew.

Not Sigurd.

And not me.

I'd expected the training to be near impossible for me. I'd run track in high school, but I wasn't some athletic woman who'd practiced martial arts and run marathons on the weekends. I was a sixth-grade math teacher turned financial advisor who preferred mimosas and charcuterie boards over weight-lifting and cardio. I did the occasional yoga workout, but I wasn't a small woman by anyone's standards. I was tall and soft. I wasn't weak, but I wasn't winning any bodybuilding contests.

On Earth, that hadn't been a problem. But that tiny blue dot was lightyears away now. And while Xavier had appreciated my softness and flexibility, Sigurd could care less.

"Focus, Lady Kyra!"

He swung his padded staff, whacking me once on the shoulder. I winced and stumbled back, glaring at him as he aimed the end of his staff at my chest.

"Was that necessary?" I mumbled, pushing the end of his staff away from me and hissing at the twinge of pain that lingered in my shoulder. I'd have an angry bruise there for days.

"Yes." He pulled his staff back and set the end on the ground. "Venra may be strengthening your body, but you need to strengthen your mind," he said. "You expect me to go easy on you because you're new to this, but there are no second chances in a fight," he pointed out, stepping back and dropping into an attack stance.

"You *could* go easy on me," I sighed, adjusting my grip on my own staff and mimicking his stance. "I wouldn't mind."

"Then how would you get any better?" he asked, lunging forward as I defended against his strike. "I do not wish to lose another captain. So," he said, pushing me back and landing three more hits against my ribs before sweeping my feet and sending me crashing to the ground, "we practice like every fight is real. Until you can hold your own against me. Now get up," he said, stepping back to his original spot as I struggled to my feet. "We go again. And this time, stay focused on my actions, not my words."

I groaned but did as I was told.

Regardless of how unenthused I was about training, I couldn't deny the truth in his words. Between Sigurd's training, Venra's injections, and the changes in my diet since leaving Earth, my body was changing — getting stronger, leaner. I had to relearn all that it could do. And Sigurd was adamant that I rely on my brain rather than some acquired ultra instinct. My gut reactions were only as effective as I learned to listen to them.

That led to me putting in long hours training with him, but not so many that I forgot about Pia or gave up on looking for her.

I found her in the dining hall one day after practice. Sigurd was with me because, while I found that he was a serious cyborg, he wasn't unlikable — he just didn't condone the kind of wallowing I had done. And I couldn't really blame him for that. It was almost natural for him to be around me now.

Almost.

He had the kind of presence I couldn't seem to overlook. I always knew when he was nearby. And, sometimes, that was exhausting. There were times I avoided him to get a break — times when he returned to Sector 10 and I was blissfully left to my own devices. It wasn't always that way, but when I found Pia, I couldn't help but focus on his presence a half-step behind me. They weren't exactly fond of each other, so I tried to ignore him as I called out to her.

She turned to meet my gaze, and the corner of her lips twitched upward until her eyes landed on Sigurd. She took one look at us together, rolled her eyes in the way only an annoyed fifteen-year-old could, and sprinted in the opposite direction, drawing every eye as she rushed out of the dining hall.

I could've caught up to her — especially with the training I'd been doing — but I'd never believed in chasing after someone who didn't want to be caught. So I let her go.

"She probably thought you were like her," Sigurd said, rolling his eyes. When I lifted my eyebrows at him, he clarified. "Self-pitying," he said. "Your grief may have dropped her into your orbit, but she was always going to fall out of it if that's all you two had in common," he said, accepting a tray of food from Sam, the tentacled alien behind the counter who worked in the kitchens. "She's realizing that."

I mulled over his words as I accepted my own tray from Sam and followed Sigurd to an empty table. I wanted to contradict his words, but I had no rebuttals. In all the time Pia and I had talked, it had never been about anything other than the past.

She didn't dream.

That stung my heart in tender places, but it wasn't something I could do anything about.

Not right now.

My own grief was still too raw.

I couldn't save her when I was still busy trying to save myself.

But once I did, I'd come back for her. I'd help her fight all the demons dragging her down into the depths of misery and set her free.

Because she deserved to revel among the stars just as much as I did.

17 CYCLES TO ZAIGERA

Once my sessions with Venra were done, and my sessions with Sigurd became light work, I acquired a weapon from Chise. It was a beautiful black staff with a hidden blade on the end that curved — morphing it into a scythe with a simple twist of my hand. It was lightweight and broke down into four parts that could shrink and bend to clasp around my wrist like an unassuming bracelet.

"This is amazing," I whispered, grinning at Chise. "Thank you."

"Thank Pia," she said. "Design was all her work. She calls it a stythe."

"She designs weapons?"

Chise nodded. "Almost every weapon on board. Siggy handles the shields. I oversee them both and keep this ship running like it's supposed to."

"Siggy?" I repeated, laughing. "Never would've thought to give him a nickname like that."

It was Chise's turn to laugh. The sound was big and deep and rumbled from the center of her chest. It reminded me of snapped peas on front porches, collard greens, and faded pink house slippers. Of grilled hotdogs, ice cold sodas, and screen doors slamming shut. Her laugh was the familiar sound of music that spanned generations. And I couldn't help but smile back at her when she grinned at me.

"I've known him since he was just a boy. All flesh, no bolts." She shook her head. "Still too small for a big name like his."

"I can't imagine that."

"Grow your imagination then," Chise said, chuckling and tapping my forehead with a chubby finger. "You ain't the only one with a past on this ship, Lady Kyra. Ain't the only one with a future either."

"You're right," I agreed, my face warming as she humbled me. "I'll be sure to thank Pia for this once she starts speaking to me again," I said, holding up my new staff and glancing over to her empty workstation.

"Give her some time," Chise hummed. "She's a delicate girl, that one."

I nodded. "Mind if I borrow Sigurd to test this thing out?"

"Take him," Chise said, waving her hand through the air as she spun her hover chair around to face her own workstation. "Ever since he's been training with you, he's been mouthing off less to me."

"I've tried to beat some sense into him for you," I quipped, and was rewarded with another one of Chise's big, rolling laughs.

"Well, keep doing it," she said. "It makes my life easier, that's for sure."

4 CYCLES TO ZAIGERA

"Let me ask you a question, Siggy."

Sigurd's sharp blue gaze shot up to mine at the nickname and I bit back the laughter that wanted to escape at the way confusion, realization, and irritation raced over his features in rapid succession. My amusement was still clear though, and he narrowed his gaze at me.

"Who —?"

"That's irrelevant," I said, pulling my hand through the air and dismissing his question before he could ask it. "Let's focus on what I want."

Sigurd sighed and pinched the bridge of his nose. "And that would be?"

"Answers," I said, leaning back against the wall. "About you and Pia."

"We're not interesting enough to ask questions about."

"Don't you want the captain of the ship to know her crew?"

Sigurd let out another deep sigh before closing his eyes and pulling a hand over his face. We'd taken a break from our training session so that I could catch my breath. I was getting better each day, but I was still a long way off from keeping pace with Sigurd. That was evident from the sweat that dripped off my face and made my shirt cling to my lower back when Sigurd wasn't so much as winded. He sipped from his bottle of water before releasing a final sigh and sinking to the ground next to me.

He sighed a lot.

"Fine," he said. "Three questions. That's it."

"How did you and Pia become Chise's apprentices?" I asked, hoping the question was broad enough to have him filling in the blanks of half a dozen questions he wouldn't answer individually. "Pia's only fifteen."

"You're asking me to tell a story that isn't mine," he said, shaking his head. "If you want to know how Pia joined the crew, ask her. But I became Chise's apprentice when I was ten, and I've known her all my life. She designed ships for my family's conglomerate during the day and bet on the hyperway races at night. She modified most of the ships she bet on herself, so she won big a lot. But one night, she lost a bet and subsequent fight with what you would call a loan shark," he said, glancing over to me. "Refused to pay up cause they cheated. Everyone saw it. As if adding a nose extender to a GX '63 Glider wouldn't be obvious," he said, snorting at the memory and rolling his eyes. "But nobody cared. Not enough to defend her. And so, they cracked her spine in three places. Took my eyes cause I saw the whole thing and beat me for good measure cause Chise tried to stop them." He scoffed at the memory and shook his head. "My parents pieced us back together with spare parts, but we were no good to them after that. Chise couldn't walk anymore and lost her reputation once her gambling was made public, and a cyborg was no good as an heir or a son. So we went to the docks and boarded the first ship that would take us both."

"And that's how you met Xavier?" I asked, my eyes wide as I tried to make sense of his story.

Chise had told me that Sigurd had a past, but I couldn't have imagined anything as gruesome as what he so casually described. But then again, she had told me to grow my imagination. I was beginning to understand what she meant now.

"It was just James and Xavier back then," he said, the ghost of a smile flitting across his lips. "They'd hitched a ride to Thrulasti and used the last of their credits to purchase *The Reveler*. Back then, it was nothing more than a tiny patchwork ship. An old prototype of Chise's my parents didn't think would sell, so they scrapped it. But Chise kept the designs and offered to modify the ship if they bought the materials and let us sail with them. And the rest is what you see," he said, gesturing around. "The ship's been upgraded countless times over the years, gotten some proper maintenance, new parts, and we've added about two dozen people to our team, but this," he said, tapping the ground with mild affection, "is our handiwork."

"That's kind of amazing," I admitted, looking around the ship with new appreciation. "I'd never have thought you would've built all this."

"You didn't ask."

"You didn't give me many opportunities to," I pointed out. "You don't like it when I ask questions."

"I don't like it when you pry," he corrected. "Being curious and nosey are two different things."

"I see someone picked up some new words on Earth."

"We were based there for twelve years," he reminded me. "It was bound to happen."

"I guess I was holding you guys back."

Sigurd nodded. "It's a crappy planet, but Captain Zay loved it because you were there. We were never going to leave Star Prime 1307 for good until you came with us."

"You don't sound happy about that."

"There's nothing to feel a way about. It is what it is," he said, throwing out another familiar phrase with a smirk. "I was just glad Captain Zay was happy."

I didn't have much to say in response to his words. An apology for the wait would've been disingenuous. I knew they'd only stopped on Earth to sightsee for a few days before leaving for their next job. Xavier had said as much when he'd asked for directions to the library — that he was just passing through.

But his plans changed after he met me. There wasn't much else that could be said, knowing that.

"You've been around a long time if you've been with James and Xavier since the beginning," I whispered, my eyebrows pulling together as I stared out across the training hall and tried to get our conversation back on track. "Do people just stop aging when they board *The Reveler*?"

"Is that your final question?"

"No," I said, shaking my head. "I was actually just thinking to myself that time."

"Then what is your final question?" Sigurd asked, lifting a brow. "We need to get back to training."

"About Pia…"

"I already told you to ask her," Sigurd said. The tiny bit of warmth that had allowed him to open up to me, slipped away and returned him to his normal frosty demeanor. "I'm not divulging someone else's secrets."

"I don't want her secrets," I said, trying to coerce him to keep talking and tell me what I wanted to know. "I just want to know how a fifteen-year-old gets put in charge of weaponry. Especially on a ship this large." When Sigurd remained tight-lipped, I sighed and shook my head. "Please," I whispered. "I'm just trying to understand this ship the best way I can."

"Talent and nepotism," Sigurd said, standing up and putting physical distance between us. "She's a genius with her hands and Chise raised her. That's all you're getting out of me," he warned. "Now get up. If you have time to be curious," he said, narrowing his eyes at the word, "you have time to practice."

"You'd think you were the captain of this ship, the way you boss me around," I muttered, pushing myself to my feet and grabbing my padded staff.

"And you'd think you were still on Star Prime 1307 with how slowly you move," he said, prodding me lightly in the back with the end of his staff and earning a scowl from me as I swatted the end of it away.

"Stop that!"

"Then get a move on," he urged, jogging to the center of the training hall. "The stars are beautiful, Lady Kyra, but they can be unforgiving. Death lingers among them if you're not careful. You have to stay ready," he warned, dropping into his fighting stance. "Now, come at me!"

1 CYCLE TO ZAIGERA

"Here."

Before I could understand what was happening, Pia was pushing off the wall beside my room and thrusting a tiny metal device into my hands. It was matte black with an extended piece on the end made of something shimmery that turned purple in the light. I frowned at it before closing my fist around it and looking up at Pia, who was already trying to make a hasty retreat.

"Wait a second," I called after her, grabbing her arm and tugging her to a stop. "You can't just shove something at me and then leave. What is this?"

"Translator," she said, refusing to meet my gaze. "You hate wearing yours, so I improved it."

"Improved it?" I repeated, glancing down at the tiny device. "Improved it how?"

When I'd been lost in the haze of Glupin's smoke, I'd often slipped the little earpiece off and left it on the bench in the observatory. I'd always had big ears, and the tiny device was irritating at best, painful at worst. James had warned me to keep it on so I could understand everyone on the ship, but that had seemed pointless, especially when I'd spent all my time in the observatory. Pia spent most of her life on Earth, so she spoke English as well as I did — along with a dozen other languages I'd never heard of before boarding *The Reveler* — but that also meant I hadn't needed the translator when I'd been talking to her.

It wasn't until I'd started training with Sigurd and studying with James that I felt the need to actually wear the thing. They spoke English too, but unlike Pia, it wasn't their preferred language. If it wasn't absolutely necessary to communicate with me, they never used it. So I'd accepted the device as a necessary evil, but it was disconcerting to have a dozen voices being translated into my ear at all times. Between the studying and the training though, I'd never thought to ask if the translator could be modified. So I didn't quite know what to make of the device in my hands now.

"For one," Pia said, letting her violet eyes dart to my face before looking away again, "it doesn't go around your ear like the old one. It goes through it," she said, pointing to her own ear where she sported a similar device in pink, "since you already have a hole there. And it's made of flexi-comozilant." When I raised my eyebrows at her in obvious confusion, she sighed. "It's super strong and basically weightless. It shouldn't break or bother you as much as the other one does."

"That's thoughtful of you," I whispered, lifting my brows in surprise. "I thought you hated me."

"What? Why?" Pia asked, her round face twisting in confusion.

"You've been avoiding me," I pointed out, releasing her arm to take the back off the translator and slide it through my tragus. I hadn't worn any kind of jewelry in months — I'd left everything but my wedding ring and the necklace my parents gave me on my thirtieth birthday in my jewelry box back on Earth. So, I was glad to find the hole hadn't closed.

"Well?" Pia asked, ignoring my statement. Her violet eyes scrutinized me as she tilted her head to get a better look at it. For a second, I caught a glimpse of the genius that lurked beneath her perpetually annoyed pout. "How's it feel?"

"Like it's not even there," I admitted, both surprised and impressed. "Works like a charm."

"Whether it worked or not was never the question," Pia said, rolling her eyes. "But I'm glad it's better than your other one."

"It is," I said, nodding. "Thanks."

"You're welcome." She gave a quick nod and a tight smile. "I'm going to go now."

"Hold up," I said, reaching for her again, but refraining from grabbing her arm when she tensed up. "Are you mad at me?"

"No?"

"You sure? Cause I haven't seen you in a while," I said, shrugging. "And this ship isn't that big."

"This ship is huge."

"You know what I mean, Pia," I said, rolling my eyes. "If you don't want to talk to me anymore, that's fine. Just say that."

"It's not like that," Pia said, crossing her arms. "I just had a bunch of work. Fixing things on the ship. Designing your new stythe. Fixing your translator," she said, pointing to my ear. "I have a job, you know? And, no offense, but everything's not about you, Lady Kyra."

Those last words were accompanied by an eye roll and all the judgment of an annoyed fifteen-year-old — they cut deep. I was twice her age and here she was, lecturing me on the responsibility of having a job and reminding me to curb my conceitedness. It was like I'd tripped into an alternate reality or something. I knew I hadn't imagined her avoiding me — everyone in the cafeteria had seen her sprint away from me — but I also knew that sometimes things had to be resolved in their own time. And whatever Pia was dealing with, it would take more than a passing conversation in the hallway to get to the root of it.

I understood that, but it frustrated me to no end to let the conversation go. I wanted to drag her to the observatory, sit her down, and force her to spill all her secrets so that I could help her through whatever was plaguing her — shake her until all her problems fell out and I could see exactly what she was dealing with. But teenage girls are complicated, no matter what planet they come from, and I accepted that getting answers from her wouldn't be that simple.

I'd only get them if she wanted to talk to me. And acting like an overprotective mother wasn't the solution either of us wanted. So, despite my desire to do otherwise, I just nodded, accepting the half-truths she offered me.

"You're right. Guess I was thinking too much into it," I said, holding my hands up in surrender. "You were busy. I can respect that."

"Thanks," she said, her shoulders visibly dropping away from her ears as I relinquished my need to have her explain herself. "I'll…" she shrugged, and glanced away from me, "I'll try to make some time to see you more often."

"I'd like that," I said, accepting her peace offering.

"Cool." She nodded and turned to leave but stopped herself mid-stride and spun back around to face me. "Oh, and before I forget, you should know I gave your translator an upgrade," she said, smirking when I lifted my eyebrows again and touched a finger to the tiny device now in my ear.

"How so?"

"James will know what I'm talking about."

"What does that mean, Pia?"

"Talk to James," she said, turning around again and jogging down the hallway toward Sector 10. "And," she paused and glanced over her shoulder, her hand resting against the wall that curved toward the hidden door at the end, "good luck, Lady Kyra. I know I'm not the only one who wants to see that man dead."

ARRIVAL ON ZAIGERA

"On your left. That's him."

I glanced in the direction James indicated to the grungy-looking man on the other side of the park. His gray shirt had most likely been white at some point and his pants had the kind of holes in them that had never been, and would never be, fashionable. His beard was split in half, covering only his cheeks and thinning before it met in the middle, as if each side were disgusted by the cracked lips of his mouth. His brown skin was ashen, and he sat on a bench, shoving a sandwich into his face and leaving all kinds of crumbs on his beard and clothes.

I'd expected to be filled with a burning rage when I laid eyes on him, but instead, I felt cold.

Everything in me went numb, and I couldn't pull my eyes away from the man. During my training sessions with James where he'd taught me to read maps and recognize the controls for *The Reveler*, he'd also given me all the information he knew about Xavier's murderer. The man we were looking for on Zaigera was a human named Howard Wright. Once a trusted member of the KUAF, he'd abandoned his position within the organization a year ago. The Known Universe's Allied Federation was comprised of planetary representatives who dedicated time and resources to keeping the established space routes and planets within the Known Universe safe. But Howard Wright had forsaken that mission. There were rumors that he still swung through the stars under a different banner — one raised by a man known only as Epidemic.

It sounded like a bad stage name to me, but James assured me that he was no laughing matter. Like everywhere else, where there were those who wanted to live in peace, there were those who thrived in chaos — those who needed to degrade others to convince themselves they stood above the rest. Epidemic was one such man. He roamed the stars, stealing from transport vessels, selling people into systems of oppression on foreign planets, and killing anyone who got in his way.

One of his crews had targeted *The Reveler* on their last transport mission, and Xavier had been the sole casualty of that conflict. That information had shocked me, but James had refused to tell me how Xavier had fallen — why he hadn't been able to defend himself against a weak man like Howard Wright. I'd been furious, but I set aside my desire for answers and funneled my rage into the task set before me.

There would be time to question James later. And this moment required my attention more than the questions swirling in my mind.

Zaigera was a beautiful planet. As much of a utopia as I'd always imagined one to be — tall trees of every color, lush green grass, a bustling city with gorgeous buildings reaching for the sky. Rails carried people with brown skin, mint-green hair, and silver eyes every which way above us and the dozens of ships docked at the landing bay beside us came in every shape, size, and color. It was my first time off *The Reveler*, but it took only a single moment for me to realize how much I'd been missing by cooping myself up inside.

I vowed never to do it again.

Today would mark the end and the beginning of an era. It had to.

So, I had to stay focused.

I closed my eyes, swept my mind of every irrelevant thought, and counted my breaths.

One, two, three, four…

In the days I'd spent with James in the control room, I'd learned a lot about the planets we traversed. I still had a lot to learn about the Known Universe, but I knew everything I needed to about Zaigera. It was lush, quiet, and it had rejected the opportunity to join the KUAF. Which meant there was no intergalactic law enforced on the planet — no extradition treaties had been signed. There was a continued era of peace on Zaigera — one that had lasted over eight hundred years. They accomplished that by minimizing their contact with outsiders. They had one docking harbor, strict borders within which visitors could travel, and even stricter laws. Theirs was a planet with no tolerance for violence of any kind. So my mission was sure to get me, and everyone else aboard *The Reveler*, banned from ever returning.

I could live with that, though.

Eleven, twelve, thirteen, fourteen, fifteen…

"What happens once I kill him?" I asked, muttering the question under my breath, knowing James would hear me. Pia's little upgrade to my translator was significant — it allowed the control center of *The Reveler* to track my location and communicate with me. It had me feeling very much like an undercover assassin as I walked through Zaigera's picturesque park. "Will that be the end of things?"

Twenty, twenty-one, twenty-two...

"If you want it to be, it will."

"And if I don't?"

"Howard's a grunt," James stated. "He pulled the trigger, but he didn't give the order. So it all depends on if you want to hunt bigger game or not."

"And if I do?"

"Then I'll make arrangements."

I nodded. The thought of collecting every blood debt owed Xavier enticed me.

"I want everyone involved to burn."

"Then we'll set the universe on fire, Ky."

Thirty-three, thirty-four, thirty-five...

"He's within range," I said, sucking in a deep breath to steady my rushing thoughts.

"You're ready for this?"

"Yes," I said, nodding. More to reaffirm my own resolve than assure James.

"You know what to do then."

"Yes," I said again. "I'll meet you back at the ship."

The line went silent, and I glanced back toward the docks, where

The Reveler waited.

Even with its strict rules and limited access, Zaigera still managed to be a hub of activity. Most of the ships docked alongside *The Reveler* originated in Zaigera, but a few were like us — from outside Zaigera's galaxy and there to either restock, recharge, or recruit new members. It was a busy center of colliding bodies, but most people never left the docks. Outside the epicenter full of merchants, shoppers, and sparse travelers, it was quiet. It gave me plenty of time to collect and quiet my thoughts as I approached Howard, tapping him on his shoulder.

He spun around and I saw the confusion cross his face at seeing another human as far away from Earth as he was — most humans didn't even know aliens were real, let alone travel into space with them. Or maybe he was surprised that anyone wanted to speak to him at all. I doubted there were many people eager to strike up a conversation with him. He seemed down on his luck, but I was incapable of feeling any pity for him. As far as I was concerned, he was a disgusting man who deserved every bit of misfortune that had befallen him.

Forty-eight, forty-nine, fifty...

"Are you Howard Wright?"

"Who's asking?"

"My name is Kyra Johnson," I said, introducing myself as I slid my bracelet from my wrist.

"Doesn't ring a bell," he said, narrowing his murky brown eyes at me. "What do you want?"

"To collect a debt," I said, staring at his face as I extended my staff and twisted, releasing the curved blade behind his head. "You killed my husband, Xavier."

"Oh, sh—"

I yanked the blade towards me before Howard Wright could finish his sentence, cutting through flesh, muscle and bone in one swift motion.

Fifty-nine.

It was harder than I'd expected, but not so hard that I couldn't do it with the enhanced strength I'd acquired from Venra. It was sickening to watch, but also… satisfying. And it concerned me that I felt relieved — almost joyous — at seeing his head plop onto the ground and roll away from his body.

In less than a minute of laying eyes on this man, I'd taken my first steps down this path of revenge.

Alarms went off before I could process what I'd done though, and I sucked my teeth as I slapped my stythe back onto my wrist, gripped Howard's head in both hands, and sprinted toward the ship. It was still leaking blood by the time I made it back to the docks, and I caught more than my fair share of terrified and disgusted looks — garnered more than a few screams of horror and heard a dozen different commands to stop — but I didn't slow down as I shoved my way forward.

The only problem was that the docks were a maze. Filled with identical roads cluttered with people, shops, wide intersections and narrow alleys, it was easy to get turned around and disoriented. I'd had no problems walking through them to the park — I'd been able to take my time and consult the maps as many times as I needed to. Now, I didn't have the luxury of time.

I could sense the enforcement squad pressing closer, trying to cut me off, and I was grateful for my training with Sigurd. Running from him during training had taught my body what to do. So, when the officer closest to me swung his club with abandon, I ducked and was able to spin away from him and keep running.

But now I was running in the wrong direction, and my heart was kicking against my ribs like a wild dog trying to escape its cage. I could barely suck in a full breath, but I couldn't stop. If I did, I'd be caught and imprisoned on Zaigera, and there was no way I'd ever see the light of any sun ever again — not when I was an alien woman who'd broken Zaigera's one cardinal rule and had tried to make off with a bloody trophy.

"There's a door on your right. Push through it and go down the stairs."

"Wha—"

"Trust me!"

The voice in my head was unfamiliar — I couldn't recognize it over the rushing of blood in my ears and the panic swirling in my chest. But I didn't have time to question it — whether I was going crazy or my guardian angel was talking to me for the first time, didn't matter. I gripped the head in my hands and did as I was told, throwing my shoulder into the first door I saw.

It didn't budge.

My shoulder throbbed, but I could hear the steps of the enforcement squad coming closer, so I gritted my teeth and threw my shoulder against it again. Some of the wood splintered, but the door held, and my heart was in my throat. My vision was spinning and my entire body felt like it was vibrating, but I refused to give up when I'd already come so far. So, I sucked down a shaky breath and threw my back into the door, forcing all my weight onto it.

It cracked and gave way, and I stumbled down a flight of clay steps into a dimly lit den filled with lanterns giving off a dingy gold light, low rising tables covered in checkered cloths and sweet smelling fruits, and a bar lining the wall in the back. The room was empty, and I was grateful for that as I stumbled through, searching for an exit of some kind.

"Where am I?" I whispered, my voice shaking and hoarse as I reached out to the voice in my head for further instruction.

"Cremlin's."

The voice that answered me was gruff, and I nearly jumped out of my skin as I turned to face the low counter of the bar. In the shadows behind it sat a man with leathery brown skin, heavy-lidded silver eyes, and mint-green hair that was balding at the crown. His knees were almost pressed to his chest with the way he sat, but he seemed unbothered by it.

"What's a girly like you doing down here?"

"I…" Words failed me, and I gulped down the muggy air of the basement as I shook my head.

"Tell him you're Xavier's wife," James said, his baritone voice a familiar sound in my ears as I released a heavy sigh of relief.

"I'm Kyra Johnson," I told the man. "Xavier's wife."

"*The Reveler*, eh?" The man lifted up out of his folded over position to appraise me in the dim light. "I heard he'd taken a wife. Settled in some backwater galaxy. But you…" he shook his head and revealed a gap-toothed grin, "you don't look the type to go reveling in them stars, missy."

"I'm bringing death to a few of them right now," I said, holding up Howard Wright's head. "For stealing his light."

"Xavier was a good man," he nodded. "Sailed with him a few years before settling here."

"Oh," I answered, glancing behind me at the door where I could hear the enforcement squad closing in and shouting to each other. "That's nice."

"It is," the man nodded again, his movements slow, as if we had all the time in the universe for this conversation. "I owed him a dozen favors or more. I take it you want to cash in on a few right now?"

"Yes, please," I answered, nodding my head as I inched further away from the door.

"Head on to the back then," the man said, jerking his chin to the door behind him. "There's a window in the storeroom. I won't tell nobody you been through."

"Thank you!"

Almost as soon as I closed the door to the storeroom behind me, heavy boots pounded on the floor. I held my breath and pressed my back to the door as they questioned the old man, Cremlin.

"Did you see an alien woman pass through here?"

"Don't open for another four gaizents, so can't say I did," Cremlin answered, his words just as lazy as our conversation moments ago. "Been chewing preenies all morn' though," he chuckled. "Prolly couldn't tell you if *you* been through here or not."

"Get a move on, Ky."

James' voice was back in my head, and it startled me back to reality.

I don't know if I would ever get used to hearing someone else's voice in my head, but I knew better than to argue. So, I swallowed my rebuttal and moved to the back of the storeroom, navigating the maze of boxes, shelves, and miscellaneous items as I inched my way closer to the dusty window that was letting in a few streaks of light. When I reached it, I sighed in relief, only to have my heart drop to my knees.

"It's locked from the outside," I whispered.

"Are you sure?" James questioned.

"There is a bar going across the window," I answered, panic pitching my voice higher. "Who locks a window from the outside? That's just stupid!"

"You can just break the window and unlock it."

"They'll hear me! The enforcement squad is already here."

"You either break the window or wait for them to find you, Ky," James said, his words sharp as steel. "You can't just stay there."

"Use the end of your stythe," a new voice interjected.

"Pia?" I questioned, my brows pulling together as my brain connected her voice to the one from earlier and I tried to make sense of why she'd be in the control center. "Why are you there?"

"Troubleshooting the equipment," she answered, without missing a beat. "Now focus. On the bottom of your stythe, there's a pommel to balance out the weight of the blade. It should be able to smash through any glass, no problem."

"And you need to be quick about it," James added. "The enforcement squad isn't dumb."

"That's really not helping," Pia snapped at James, before steadying her voice. "Just break the window, Lady Kyra. Break it. Unlock it. Get back to the ship. Easy."

Pia made it sound like a cakewalk, and I let loose a string of curses before closing my eyes and clearing my mind. My brain was screaming at me that there was no time to breathe, but I knew that if I didn't take the time now, I'd wish I had later. And having a focused mind was better than relying on pure adrenaline to tell me what to do. So, after three quick breaths, I set Howard Wright's head aside, pulled off my bracelet, and gripped the extended staff with both hands.

"Alright," I whispered. "Here goes."

I slammed the end of the pommel into the window and it cracked beneath the pressure, but it didn't shatter. It did, however, alert the enforcement squad to my location, and I tried to ignore them as my pulse pounded in my ears and I slammed the end of the staff against the glass twice more. It finally fell from the pane just as the door to the storeroom crashed open.

"Stop right there!"

I refused to look behind me as I focused on using the blade of my stythe to shove the bar blocking the window out of the way.

It slipped over the curved edge of the blade and fell back into place and I fought back tears of panic as I cursed and tried again. The second time it fell away, and it was with shaking hands that I forced the squeaky window frame open, tossing Howard Wright's head through first before hoisting myself up onto the ledge.

I was almost through it when one of the enforcement squad grabbed my ankle. I screamed in surprise and tried to kick free of him, but he held tight, as if I was his only lifeline out of hell.

And he was strong.

He started yanking me back inside and I scrambled for something to grab onto. The first thing my fingers touched was my stythe and without thinking, I shoved it behind me, slamming the pommel into the center of the man's face with all the force I could muster.

He screamed and jolted backwards. I seized the opportunity to scoop up Howard Wright's head and resume sprinting through Zaigera's streets. Another squad member raced through the broken door of the bar and chased after me, but I was running off pure adrenaline and made it to the ship much faster than I would have ever thought was possible.

"Go!" I shouted into the ship, wheezing for breath as the door hissed closed behind me and I collapsed to the ground. "Takeoff! Now!"

"You heard the captain," James said, echoing my command. "Let's go!"

2 DAYS
A LADY

The head of Howard Wright now sat enclosed in a cryogenic case in the control center. I didn't know who put it there, but until we reached the planet Shereve in the Minotosah Galaxy, there it would remain.

James had heard rumors of a specialist who could access the memories of the dead — as long as their brain was still intact. It was no one he'd met, but their location was a well-known secret — a story that's never been written but has been passed on from captain to crew and between travelers for centuries. He'd had the triplets input the location the second we'd taken off from Zaigera. It would take a few months to reach Shereve, so for now, Howard Wright was nothing more than a bloody trophy — one James encouraged me to turn in for a reward once we got the information we needed.

Howard's bounty was small, but it would be enough to establish some credits in my own name. Not that I needed them. Xavier had left me everything he had — I could live twice as long as he did and still never work another day in my life. But making money off the man who'd killed him seemed right — like I was owed for what he took from me.

And I would collect.

Until I did though, his severed head would serve as proof to everyone that I was more than just a broken woman left behind by their captain.

I was more than just Xavier's widow now.

I was *Lady Kyra.*

The Lady Widow.

I'd taken the first step in avenging my husband, and it might've just been in my head, but I felt like the crew looked at me with a little more respect in their eyes. Even I looked at myself a little differently now. But I knew vengeance had come at a steep price. There was no telling what damage had been done to my soul, but whatever the cost, I was happy to pay it.

If it meant James could make peace with Xavier's death.

If it meant I could face a future without him.

It wouldn't be easy. I wasn't fool enough to believe I was fully healed from this hurt, but I knew I had to keep pushing forward. Howard Wright was just the first in a long line of people who needed to die by my hand, and I wasn't going to allow them to keep roaming the stars like nothing had happened when my husband lay rotting in Earth's crust. It would take time for me to figure everything out — and there was a lot I still needed to learn.

But I wasn't alone.

And maybe that's why Xavier left *The Reveler* in my care to begin with. And why James had been patient and kept his word — because they knew I'd arrive here in my own time.

They'd brought me to the stars, and I'd call this ship my home.

I'd start my adventure where Xavier's ended.

I'd collect the head of every person who worked to steal my husband away from me.

And I would make sure they knew nothing but death among the stars.

THE LADY WIDOW

BOOK 2 PREVIEW

13 DAYS A LADY

"I thought you'd given up smoking in the observatory?"

I opened my eyes and let them roam over Sigurd. His six-two frame filled the small doorway by the stairs as he studied me with crossed arms. Part of me wanted to explain myself — that I'd just come up here to get a break from him and James and their hellish training. But that explanation wouldn't go over well with him and a much larger part of me enjoyed pushing his metaphorical buttons and watching the bright blue hues of his cybernetic eyes and joints light up with frustration. So, I smiled and shrugged at him instead.

"Aw. You worried about me, Siggy?"

"Don't call me that."

"You love that name," I said, laughing as I struck a match and fed it to Glupin. When he didn't move to sit down, I rolled my eyes and gestured to the free seat across from me. "You can sit down, you know. This is only his second match, and I haven't fed him in over ten cycles.

It's fine."

"He?" Sigurd asked, lifting his brows as his lips twitched. "You can tell them apart now?"

"Yes?"

I frowned, unsure of what Sigurd meant. Glupin had always seemed like an it before — more an orange plushie rather than a living being — but the more time I spent with Glupin, the less he felt like a thing and more like a companion. It didn't feel right to keep objectifying him. Not when he clearly liked me and glubbed so sweetly whenever I held onto him and squished his little form in my hands. He was adorable and loyal, and I loved him.

"I mean, Glupin is clearly a boy."

"Sure he is," Sigurd chuckled. "If you say so."

"Can you tell them apart?" I asked, feeling irritated by Sigurd's smug attitude.

"Slimes don't take on a gender until they bond with a host," he stated, moving to sit on the bench next to me and stretch out his long legs in front of him. "And then they take on whatever gender their host sees them as. So, if you say Glupin is a boy," he said, squishing his fingers gently into Glupin's round form as he glubbed out a fresh stream of smoke, "he's a boy. You would know better than anyone else."

"That's kinda cool," I said, grinning at Glupin as I picked him up. "I didn't know that about you."

He glubbed again and the smoke in the room smelled of warm apple cider, cinnamon, freshly baked bread and cream cheese icing. I inhaled a deep breath and smiled at the memory of warm cinnamon rolls that Glupin gave me. I sank into it for a moment, closing my eyes and drifting back to softer days of baking in my kitchen, wearing cozy sweaters, and sipping spiked cider with Xavier. Moments like that were what I missed most about him sometimes. And though I was grateful to Glupin for breathing life back into the memories for me, sometimes, my throat got thick thinking of what would never be again.

It was better some days, but others I'd be left a blubbering mess and, for once, I was glad that I wasn't alone — that Sigurd was with me. He wasn't my favorite person on the ship, but we understood each other. Quiet moments with him were always comfortable rather than awkward.

He never felt the need to fill the silence with pointless chatter.

So, I took a moment to let myself breathe through the memory. To remember Xavier and our life together. To be grateful for every moment we had and to be heartbroken over the memories we'd never be able to create. It was a process, and Sigurd sat in silence next to me as I closed my eyes and worked through the waves of emotions crashing into me.

Maybe he had his own thoughts about missing Xavier — Captain Zay, as he and the rest of the crew had known him — but we never spoke about that. And maybe that's why I appreciated the silence with Sigurd. He understood some things weren't meant to be shared with everyone. That there were some things we held on to, just for ourselves.

He never pushed, and I never pried.

We worked best like that.

Once Glupin's smoke dissipated, I turned my attention to Sigurd. He was bent over, with an elbow on his knee as he watched the stars on the display panels showing us the galaxy we drifted through. There were still more than sixty cycles left before we would reach Shereve in the Minotosah Galaxy, but the expanse of space we sailed through now was beautiful — filled with dozens of pink and purple planets. I'd done my best to identify as many of the planets as I could, but I still had a long way to go before I had a casual knowledge of them the way James did.

Thinking of him reminded me of the training I'd taken an extended break from and I stretched my arms above me as I turned to look at Sigurd.

"Why'd you come up here?" I asked. "I doubt all you wanted was my company."

"I was hoping to find Pia up here," he admitted. "But clearly she's not and isn't coming."

"She avoiding you too now?"

"Seems like it," he said, shrugging.

"I'm worried about her," I said, returning my attention to the stars. "Distancing yourself from people you care about isn't normal behavior."

"She'll be fine."

"You say that as if it doesn't matter if she won't be."

"I say that as if she's a child," he said, turning his head to look at me. "She's unmoored right now without her captain and probably frustrated that you, his wife," he said, pointedly, "is somehow dealing with his absence better than she is. But she'll bounce back soon enough."

"Will she?" I asked, shaking my head and swallowing the tears clogging my throat at the reminder that I was no longer anyone's wife. "I don't know if death is something you just bounce back from, Siggy."

"It is something that grows with you," he said, his voice gentle.

"Your world has to expand beyond the grief until it is only a part of who you are and not the entirety of your being. And lucky for you," he said, glancing at me again, "and for Pia," he added, "there's an entire universe lying in wait for you."

"That's a positive way to look at it."

"It's the only way to look at it," he corrected. "And if Pia needs our help remembering that her world is bigger than what she's feeling right now, we'll be there for her. But all we can do right now is give her some space. We can't force her to heal on our schedules."

"That's true," I conceded. "I'll be patient."

"Great," Sigurd said, reaching out to squeeze my shoulder in an awkward display of concern before dropping his hand. "If that's settled, then I'm going back to wo—"

The Reveler tilted in a way that was unnatural. Sigurd slid across the bench, his body crashing into mine as we slammed into the wall behind me. His forehead bumped into mine and we both hissed in pain as he braced himself, pressing his palms into either side of the wall behind me.

Heat rolled off his brown skin as his blue eyes darted upward. Orange lights were flashing and the same serene voice that announced our takeoffs and descents informed us that we were now under enemy fire. Sigurd sucked his teeth, and his blue eyes pinned me to the spot as he lifted his voice over the alarm.

"Where's your bracelet?"

I glanced down at my wrist and felt my heart drop. We were expected to be onboard for a few months before docking again, so I'd left Mandy — the name I'd affectionately given to my stythe — back in my room. I didn't think I'd need to carry a weapon around me onboard, so all I could do was shake my head at Sigurd.

He sucked his teeth again and sighed as the gravity control of the ship recalibrated. He pushed away from me, grabbed Glupin, and shoved him into my hands.

"Don't let go of him and follow me."

He took off jogging down the stairs, and I huffed as I pushed to my feet and stumbled across the observatory after him, the last traces of Glupin's smoke making my first few steps unsteady. But I knew he'd never slow down for me, so I sprinted down the stairs in an effort to keep up with him.

"Where are we going?"

"Control room," Sigurd shouted back, giving me a straight answer for the first time in his life. "Without Captain Zay, James can't fight."

The other questions I might have had stuck in my chest. The stories Xavier had regaled me with came flooding back through my memories, and I realized they may not have been as exaggerated as I once thought. My heart jumped into my throat at that realization and I tightened my grip on Glupin as I sped up, doing my best to keep pace with Sigurd.

"I'm behind you!"

Sigurd led us through the flurry of bodies to the control room. The crew was picking up their weapons and gathering in the atrium to wait for orders. The residents, though — they were locking their doors and shutting themselves inside their homes as giant metal doors came down in the hallways, sealing off each sector.

"What's happening?" I asked, my eyes growing wide as Sigurd and

I ducked under the door slowly sliding into place between Sector 2 and Sector 3.

"Lockdown," he answered, keeping a firm grip on my hand as he pushed our way through the crowds rushing in every direction. "It keeps the residents safe so the crew can fight."

It was a simple explanation, and I was reminded of an early lesson with James, when he'd explained the roles of everyone on the ship. The crew was necessary to keep the ship running, but the residents were what kept the finances of *The Reveler* strong. We transported people and cargo through space, and we needed the economy in Sectors 4 through 8 to keep credits flowing through the ship. A portion of every market sale went toward the ship as a sort of tax, and that kept us from being overly reliant on any one company for work. It allowed us the freedom to accept or decline whatever work requests we wanted.

If the residents died, *The Reveler* would cease to exist.

Or, at the very least, be unable to travel through space with as much ease as we did now. But financial logistics aside, none of us wanted to see anyone on the ship get hurt. So, the lockdown procedures were in place to keep everyone safe. If anyone did breach the ship, they'd be met in Sector 10 and funneled to either Sector 9 or Sector 1 — away from any stragglers who may not have gotten back home before their Sector was sealed off. In those cases, most of them sought shelter in Sector 3 until the fighting was over.

It was a system that had been fine-tuned over the centuries, but it still felt like a madhouse with everyone rushing around, and my heart nearly choked me to death before we even reached the control center.

But when the doors hissed open, it was like stepping out of a burning circus into a tranquil office.

The triplets tapped away at their consoles and James stood in the center of the crescent, his hands in his pockets as he surveyed the chaos outside from a dozen different screens shifting before him. When Sigurd and I stepped inside, he grinned and stepped over to us, pulling Sigurd into one of those man hugs — the kind that's a mix between a dap and a pat on the back. It was something he had to have picked up on Earth, and it was such an unexpected normalcy, I almost felt homesick for a moment. It helped to calm my racing heart, and I followed both of them inside as James tapped on the console screen in the center — the one meant for the captain — and enlarged our view of a giant ship blocking our path forward.

It looked straight out of a sci-fi movie, with all types of hulls and thrusters and lasers, and I worked to pull in deep breaths to steady my racing heart. The ship was nothing if not intimidating, and the thought of being in a fight with them fed my anxiety in ways I didn't appreciate. But I seemed to be the only one fighting off waves of panic. Everyone else seemed calm, as if this were as routine as docking the ship at a nearby planet for lunch.

"I'm glad you're here," James said, letting his dark gaze bounce between Sigurd and me. "Although I'm a bit surprised you're together. Were you training today?"

"No," Sigurd said. When it was clear he wasn't going to elaborate further, James turned his gaze to me, and I shrugged.

"Do I need a reason to talk to someone?"

"No," James said, lifting his brows and making the word almost sound like a question. "I'm just surprised. Either way, it's convenient for me."

"What do you need?" Sigurd asked.

"For the captain to take the helm," James said, turning to face me.

"You mean me," I said, biting my lip and nodding. I'd gotten used to the title over the weeks since I'd killed Howard Wright, but it still felt too big for me. I much preferred when the crew called me the lady of the ship rather than its captain, but this was no time to be delicate about what he called me. So, I took a steadying breath and turned to meet James' gaze.

"What do you need me to do?"

"Watch everything," James said, pointing to the monitors, "and give the orders."

"What orders?"

"Whatever feels right," he said, sliding his hands back into his pockets. "I've gone over the protocols with you, and we've practiced the simulations. The only thing left is the real thing. But if you don't feel comfortable with that…"

"I'll be fine," I assured him. "This is my job. And," I said, glancing around to the three women surrounding us, "it's not like I'll be here alone."

And that much was true.

James had always believed in my ability to lead the crew — had never doubted Xavier's decision to leave me in charge of the home they'd built among the stars. But everyone hadn't shared in his sentiments, and it hadn't helped that I'd been drowning in my grief when I arrived. The triplets, especially, had been harsh doubters of my future aboard *The Reveler* and hadn't been shy about voicing their distrust of me during my training sessions with James.

Respect was a thing earned on this ship, and they'd had none to spare for me. I'd used up all the grace they'd been willing to offer me as Xavier's widow when we'd landed in the Pursinian Galaxy and I'd refused to get off the ship, defying James' warning about Glupin and nearly killing myself in the process.

It wasn't until I returned to the control center, clear-headed and with an apology, that any of them were willing to spare me a second glance. In the days that passed, I'd gotten to know Karmen, Keelah, and Kavira on an individual basis and understood that they were more than just navigators — they were the eyes, ears, and voice of the crew. And considering their role on the ship, it made sense.

From the control center, they could see every corner of the ship that wasn't a private residence. They saw the people, bore witness to their lives, listened to their woes, and advocated on their behalf when necessary. They were the intermediaries of the ship and had been fielding more than a few disgruntled and anxious complaints about the new leadership. But the rules of the ship were clear — I was the captain until I died or disbanded the crew, just as James had told me on the very first day I arrived.

So, I was determined to be better than I was.

I'd come to the control center every day. I'd studied under James, asked questions, and learned about every aspect of the ship I could. I read the maps, memorized the planets, learned about the ship, its history, and everywhere it had been. Not just so that everyone's memory of Xavier wouldn't be tainted by my failure, but because I wanted to be the leader they deserved.

If I was going to ask them to turn away from a peaceful existence of transportation and deliveries to tread one of blood and carnage, the least I could do was be reliable — understand the job and show up for work.

So, I nudged James with a sharp elbow and a tiny smirk when he lifted his brows at me in a silent question: *Are you sure?*

"I'll be fine," I repeated, placing Glupin on the edge of the center console. "Go do what you have to do. I'll be here when you get back."

"Understood," James said, stepping back from the center of the crescent and smirking at me. "Captain at the helm!"

"Captain at the helm!" the triplets repeated in unison.

With those words, Sigurd and James nodded at me, warned me to be careful, and rushed out of the room. In their absence, I was reminded that I now had direct command of the ship. That made my heart pound twice as hard in my chest, but I'd known this day would come, eventually. It was nothing like my training sessions when I had the comfort of James's presence standing next to me, but instead of falling into a panic, I pulled out the chair in the center of the console — the one meant for the captain — and sank into it.

It was huge and navy blue and still smelled faintly of Xavier.

I took a deep breath and held it in. I was both grateful that this small piece of the ship still carried the memory of him, and angry with myself for always denying his invitations for adventure. But the past would forever remain unchanged, and this wasn't the moment to lose myself to thoughts of what could have been. So, I released the breath I'd been holding and rolled back my shoulders, getting comfortable in Xavier's chair.

"I'll be relying on you three to get me through this," I said, stretching out my fingers and letting them hover over the glowing buttons as James had taught me to do. "I'll do my best not to slow you down."

"Understood. We're ready when you are, *Captain*."

It was Karmen who spoke the words, but both Kavira and Keelah nodded in unison with her. It was a small acknowledgement, but it was a huge step forward for all of us and I couldn't stop the tiny smile that pulled at the corner of my lips.

"Alright," I said, returning their nods before focusing my attention on the screens the triplets pulled up in front of me. "Then let's do it. Talk me through this."

The next twenty minutes felt like twenty years.

The triplets talked me through each scene that popped up before me — showing me first the main corridors and sectors that were locked down. We confirmed that all the travelers were safe in secured areas before moving on to Sector 10.

I'd always known the sector was huge — it served as an outer shell for the ship and it's where the engineers, mechanics, and shipwrights that Chise, Pia, and Sigurd oversaw did most of their work. Now though, it was a battlefield.

The hangar bay, where the smaller ships with lasers were stored, had been cleared out — all of them zipping and zooming through space between our ship and *The Croceria,* firing at the enemy.

Their purpose for attacking us was unclear, but their reasons could range anywhere from wanting to steal our cargo to alien trafficking. Our goal was to keep them locked down at the hangar bay and keep them from infiltrating the ship.

James and Sigurd led the charge, shouting orders, firing lasers, and ripping through our enemies. I'd never seen an intense battle where icy blue lasers were being fired and people were being vaporized in real time. My breath caught in my throat at the sight, and my eyes were saucers glued to the displays.

James and Sigurd gave orders to the crew on the front lines in the hangar bay, which left me in charge of the fighters who defended the ship's inner sectors. And each time we pushed their defensive line back, they did the same to ours, despite the skill that James, Sigurd, and the others displayed.

Minutes stretched out like eons as warriors covered in ice and pale gray scales forced their way deeper into *The Reveler,* breaking through to Sector 9 — bearing down on the second line of defenders with sharpened claws. The enemy looked like overgrown crocodiles in navy

blue tactical gear. They were powerful, but they didn't know the ship —
which worked to our benefit.

"Tell Unit C to fall back," I said, infusing my voice with more
confidence than I'd ever felt in my life. "There's an escape hatch in Sector
3," I said, glancing at the map of the ship and silently thanking Sigurd
and Chise for explaining to me how to read the pink holodisplays. "Have
them meet with Unit A there. We can seal off the corridor once they
arrive, open the hatch and yeet both sets of Crocs into space."

"What did you call them?" Kavira asked, her brown eyes dancing
over to me for a moment. "And what is a 'yeet'?"

"They're Earth terms," I said, brushing off her question. "Show
me Unit D on the south side of Sector 10," I said. "With Units A and C
freed up, we might be able to divide and conquer the Crocs that are left.
Take them three on one."

"There's not much honor in that," Keelah noted. "Playing the
numbers advantage."

"There is no honor in death," I said, keeping my tone even. "We
fight to live. Not for some misplaced ideals of glory."

"You heard her," Karmen said, speaking into the display. "Divide
and conquer! And keep your heads on your shoulders at all costs!"

The next few minutes carried on like that — with me giving orders
in an effort to keep the crew alive and the triplets conveying them. The
ship was massive though, and I felt like I was barking orders nonstop.
Most of them made sense. Some of them — like cornering the Crocs
in the sub-kitchens of Sector 9 and throwing the equivalent of hot grits
at them — were a bit unorthodox. But soon the ship was quiet again,

absent of any surviving Crocs.

I was making a final cycle through the observation displays with the triplets when a girl with a messy bun, baggy overalls, and panicked violet eyes caught my attention as she sprinted down a corridor from the mech room toward the hangar bay. A grisly Croc that was twice the size of the others lumbered down the hallway after Pia and I slammed my hands into the console as I jumped to my feet.

"Where is she?"

Everyone in the room understood my question and began swiping across their screens to give me an answer. Karmen was the first to respond.

"The west side of Sector 10."

"What is she doing all the way over there?" I asked, shaking my head. "The hangar bay is to the north. How'd it get in this far?"

"Escape hatch," Kavira said, pulling up a screen showing a hastily patched hole on the far side of the ship. "Looks like it pried it open with its claws and climbed up while everyone else was focused on the hangar bay. I don't know why the alarms didn't sound..."

"Can we get her out?" I asked. "Seal the Croc down there alone until someone can reach them?"

"Unlikely," Keelah said, shaking her head. "It would take too long to lock down Sector 10."

"Are you telling me there's no way to get her out?" I asked, scouring the holodisplay map for an exit. "There's a door not too far from where she is that leads to Sector 9."

"With all due respect, Captain," Karmen said, choosing her words with care, "that would endanger all the residents on board. It would be unwise to lead it further inside the ship."

"So, you just want to abandon her?"

"She is one crew member weighed against hundreds of non-combatants, Lady Kyra," Keelah said, her tone icy as she interjected. "This isn't what we desire, but this is the nature of being the captain of this ship," she said. "Power and privilege come with responsibility and hard decisions. This is one of them."

I bit my lip in frustration and stood in silence, thinking of all the reasons why Keelah was right. Her logic was sound. In the grand scheme of the ship, even with all her brilliance, Pia was still just one girl. And in their eyes, I'm sure she could be replaced.

But Pia was the one who had kept me company during the worst days of my life. Who had climbed the stairs of the observatory and listened to my stories of Xavier when everyone else had been content to let me rot in my misery. She was the one who'd designed and crafted a weapon meant especially for me, and she was the one who'd noticed how much I hated my translator and modified it into something I could actually use. She was the one who'd given me directions when I was running from the enforcement squad on Zaigera and she was the one who needed me the most right now.

There would always be someone looking out for the best interests of the ship.

Right now, my job was to look out for her. Because who would if I didn't?

"I understand what you're saying," I said, nodding at Keelah.

"Great," she said, sighing. "Then we can —"

"But I don't agree with it," I continued. "I'm not going to stand here and pretend I don't see her when she needs help." I shook my head. "I know you three will do what's best for the ship. Continue to do that until James return."

"And what are you going to do?" Kavira asked. "You're not a fighter, Lady Kyra."

"No, but I'm not going to just abandon her either," I said, reaching out for Glupin.

He'd been glubbing quietly on the console next to me, and with the slightest invitation, he launched into the air and crawled over my shoulder to cling to my back. He was squishy and warm and his presence startled me a bit — I didn't know slimes could jump like that — but I refused to flinch, yelp, or show any sign of weakness in front of the triplets. So, I ignored him and strode toward the exit.

"Is the gravity control still intact?"

"Yes," Karmen said. "Why?"

"I'm going to Sector 10," I stated. "And from here, it's faster if I just jump."

I didn't stay to hear any more words of dissent from the triplets.

All I had in mind were three things.

Grab my bracelet.

Find Pia.

Kill the Croc.

The tasks sounded far simpler in my head than I imagined they would actually be, but I knew that if I stopped to consider what kind of situation I was walking myself into, I'd doubt myself. I'd doubt my decision to save Pia and my ability to do it. And I didn't want that. Because even if I couldn't save her, it wouldn't be because I didn't try.

It wouldn't be because I abandoned her like the triplets seemed to be okay doing.

So, once I'd bounded out of the control room, I stepped over to the nearest railing and hoisted myself up on top of it. I'd seen others use the gravity control of the ship like a broken elevator, but jumping didn't feel any smarter when I was staring over the edge.

But the control center was in Sector 3, near the top of the ship. My room was in Sector 9 and Pia was in Sector 10. If I wanted to get to her with half the ship on lockdown, the fastest way would be to jump.

There was no time for my fear of heights to hold me back.

"You jump, I jump, Jack."

I spoke the words to no one in particular, but saying them aloud was enough to give me the burst of courage I needed to fling myself over the side.

And, at first, it was terrifying. The wind rushing through my hair and through my ears and snatching all my thoughts from me. I wanted to scream.

But instead of terror, laughter bubbled up from me.

And my eyes widened at the sound. Glupin jiggled on my back in what I could only assume was delight, and I relinquished my hold on all the things I'd been desperately clinging to for dear life.

My sanity.

My expectations.

The memories of my husband.

I was freer than I'd ever been. And something about laughing while freefalling through a spaceship in the midst of an epic space battle brought a clarity to my mind I'd never felt before.

This is what Xavier had wanted to give me.

Just being in the stars wasn't enough.

I had to revel among them.

I finally understood what that meant.

But no sooner than I'd figured that out, was I slowing down and my feet were brushing against the floor. I was on the bottom floor of *The Reveler* and there was no time to waste.

The lockdown had put most of the lights on the ship at half capacity, to conserve energy and funnel every drop of power that was needed to the ships defensive shields. Every step I took seemed to echo down the hall and a chill raced up my spine as I dashed into my room, scooping my bracelet off my desk and slapping it on my wrist.

"Now, to find Pia."

I'd barely taken two steps back into the hallway when the metal divider separating Sectors 9 and 10 screeched as a gaping hole was ripped into it. Before I could even think to scream, a scaly hand wrapped around my throat. It lifted me off my feet and slammed me into the wall behind me, knocking all the wind and good sense out of me. I felt Glupin glub and squish beneath me before it spread out, wrapping itself around my chest like a vest. I heaved and clutched at the hard, scaly hand, blinking a thousand times to try and clear my vision as the massive crocodile came into view.

It stood on two legs like a man, but it was all beast. It wore a navy-blue tactical suit like the others, but its shiny scales were pitch black and frigid against my skin. I shivered as I squirmed beneath its grasp, trying to free myself.

"Who…"

"I am Zentrith," it hissed at me. "And you've upset The Boss. So you're coming with me."

My eyes glanced around, desperate to find anyone I could call out to for help, but all I saw was Pia's slumped-over body on the ground, being dragged behind the massive crocodile by its tail. Her neck sported the same bruises I would no doubt have soon, and I tried to reach for my bracelet — for a way to fight back. But it was a pointless endeavor. Before I could, Zentrith was pulling me from the wall and hissing again.

"Enough of that. Sleep."

With that, he tightened his grip on my neck and slammed me against the wall twice more. The first time, I loosened my grip on him and my thoughts darted to Pia — how I managed to not only fail at saving her, but get myself captured, too. I almost wanted to laugh at myself. I'd tried to be a hero like Xavier and now I was either going to die or become someone's hostage.

James was going to be furious.

Zentrith slammed me into the wall again and finally — mercifully — everything went black.

TO BE CONTINUED...

C. M. Lockhart writes stories about Black girls who aren't all that nice. Her debut novel, *We Are the Origin*, was released in June 2022 and its sequel, *We Are Dying Gods*, was released August 2023. Her latest series, *The Lady Widow*, is her first venture into the sci-fi genre. She is the founder of Written in Melanin LLC, which encompasses a podcast and YouTube channel of the same name, and the Melanin Library, an online database of books written by Black authors. More information can be found on her website, https://WrittenInMelanin.com

Thank you for reading Death Among the Stars, the first book of The Lady Widow series. If you enjoyed this book, please consider telling a friend and leaving a rating or review for it on Amazon, Goodreads, Storygraph, or your favorite reading app of choice.

You can find more books by C. M. Lockhart on her website, CMLockhart.com

Special thanks to my husband, Benjamin Lockhart for reading every version of this story that ever existed; Tatiana Obey for reading this story, editing it, talking some sense into me, and being the amazing friend she is; La Purvis for being my chosen sister and kind enough to let me hog our shared brain-cell while I wrote this; Celeste Harte for being one of the first to read this story and give me her honest opinion; to all my beta readers, especially those who weren't shy about admitting I made them cry — that was more encouraging than you probably realize; to my ARC readers who helped me share this book with the world; and, lastly, I want to thank me — for seeing this book through and publishing it even when it scared it me.

I'm grateful to everyone and, until next time, I hope all your days are lovely and your books full of melanin.

www.ingramcontent.com/pod-product-compliance
Lightning Source LLC
Chambersburg PA
CBHW071936190726
48293CB00004B/1267